neighbor

neighbor
(stories)

by
will lupens

Polyho Press • Somerville, Massachusetts

Polyho Press
10 Howard Street
Somerville, Massachusetts 02144
www.polyho.com

This is a work of fiction. Names, characters, places and incidents are either the product of the author's imagination or are used ficticiously, and any resemblance to actual persons, living or dead, business establishments, events, or locales is entirely coincidental.

Collector of Worlds first appeared in The Circle.
The Not Perfectly Spherical Object first appeared in Dream Fantasy International.

Home was written for BJ. *Mist* is for Melissa; *Virus Worms* is for Jane; *Word Made Flesh v2.0* is for Allison & Jerry; *Grim(m)* is for Roanne. *Old* was written for John, in memory of his father, Stanley Chervinsky.

Copyright © 2005 by Will Lupens
Cover photograph copyright © 2005 by R. Dodson

All rights reserved. This book, or parts thereof, may not be reproduced in any form without permission.

First Polyho trade paperback edition: September 2005
First Polyho trade paperback ISBN: 0-9771557-0-6

This book was set in Warnock at Polyho Press. It was designed at Polyho Press and printed and bound by Capital City Press, Montpelier, Vermont

*These are the people you write for,
the ones who've already written you:
BJ, Melissa & Chris, Michael & Didi, Misti, David.
Randy & Lucy, Allison & Reynold, Kirstin & John,
Nancy, Rick, Dave M, Ed, Roanne, Bernard M & Jerry.
The little ones, who are better than me but like me anyway:
Maggie, Atticus, Aymara, Che, Declan & Finnea,
Zoë & Sydney, Basil & Lucy, Doc & Wilder.
My elders, in every possible way:
Judi & Joe, Jane & Tony.
Above all my brother, Scott.*

1 | *light, tunnel, etc.*
5 | *grim(m)*
15 | *sulu*
37 | *neighbor*
43 | *numb*
49 | *mother of god*
83 | *virus worms*
89 | *old*
95 | *swing*
121 | *mist*
125 | *the not perfectly spherical object*
131 | *phthalo blue*
143 | *habitat*
149 | *home*
155 | *word made flesh v2.0*
179 | *the thereminist*
183 | *2050 or, what it was like*
193 | *collector of worlds*
211 | *lint*

for
Sheila & Max
(& Will)

In the distance, suspended and without salvation, shone a dim star, and it would never be any closer.
-Andrei Platonov

light, tunnel, etc.

THE DOUBT SET IN when I realized it was unfolding exactly the way everyone says it does: the tunnel of pure light; the wash of spiritual calm; the placid beckoning—guileless, reassuring—of lost loved ones. I half-expected piped-in whale song. Even so, I ambled casually down the luminous hallway, making my way with studied indifference toward the heavenly welcome wagon.

Assembled near the center of my field of vision (for such was the tunnel, in truth) was an array of likely personages, all the obvious choices: Gran in her flannel wood-chopping shirt and navy stirrup pants, her smiling face all asquint, the silver hairs on her chin glinting in the sourceless light; Eddie Martinez as he was before his run-in with the train, leaning against his kick-standed bike in his grass-stained soccer uniform and post-game sneakers, his cleats tied together and slung over his shoulder; Father Flanagan, standing beside the open door to his study, a snifter of apricot brandy in his hand, his ruddy face puckered by its customary avuncular leer; Herbie and Harry, my goldfish, still in their five-gallon tank with its bed of orange pebbles, and still struggling against that ichthyogastric problem that always had them floating toward the surface . . .

My ambling came to a stop. There was evidence enough that this heaven was in fact a dream, a mid-brain fabrication. But that's not what stopped me. My progress was arrested, rather, by the growing suspicion that I would not be allowed to stay.

And—as if I needed further proof of the undeniably virtual nature of my surroundings—I now saw, loitering off to one side, the not-yet-dead or those whose interest in my arrival could not be easily explained: both of my fathers, standing side-by-side and holding hands; a cardiganed, ruby-lipped Mr. Rogers, winking at me slyly as he slid his windbreaker onto a wooden coat-hanger; a soft-focus Anne Margaret, pretending to be asleep in a webbed-nylon patio chair; a cowlicky, brown-haired boy, the play-worn knees of his brown canvas pants reinforced by two generations of iron-on patches.

Brown canvas pants. My pants.

I smiled at my seven-year-old self and he smiled back. His toothless grin was spread wide, though it was no match for the span of his indefatigable ears. The thing in your brain that makes you weep from happiness began filling my right eye with water. Still looking into my eyes and smiling, the other me shook his head sympathetically from side to side: *No.*

I looked at him for another moment, and another. Then, my right eye now a quivering pool, I turned away, trudging my way with grudging acceptance past a telephone pole festooned with the steaming wreck of my car and the ungrateful, chittering squirrel for whose sake I had swerved off the road.

There was light in this direction, too. The tight beam of a physician's penlight. The lid of my right eye was held open by a masculine, latexed thumb, my retina scrubbed by a shaft of ardent photons. I wanted to close my eye, it was starting to burn, but he held the lid firm, this physician, still intent on the appraisal of some optic function or other. The tears gathered in the corner of my eye spilled over at last, running across the vein that always stands out on my lower temple, only to pool once again in my ear.

The room was dark gray, everything fuzzily penumbral behind the fore-grounded doctor's pitch-black form. Finally, I could no longer bear the light and tried to look away, apparently the sign he was looking for. I heard the whisper of hushed exclamations, the rustling of clothes. Then a voice, reverberating cathedrally: *Ahhhh . . . yes. Here he is. Yes. Welcome back, Mr. Tilden . . .*

I came back.

grim(m)

Act now!!!
These were the first coherent words to pass my son's lips. Not some proto-lexic nickname for the milk-producing binary stars that were so briefly the rightful center of his universe. Not the petulant no with which the toddler so adroitly circumscribes its organic sovereignty. Not even one of those phenotypic hard palatals *(da, dada, dad)* so often mistaken for evidence of the father's exalted role in the social hierarchy.

Act Now!!!

His first words. His first complete sentence. The call-to-arms of Ron Popeil. Even then, I had mixed feelings about it.

There was embarrassment, to be sure. It was clear he was spending a little too much time in front of the television. That is, it was clear I was placing him in front of the television a little too often. Still, I couldn't help feeling a little bit of relief that, at least in the early stages of the battle for his soul, the forces of progress, however dubious, had beaten those of reaction—religion, primarily—to the punch.

I had, I told myself, a progressive outlook: television, whatever its numerous shortcomings, is at least *of our times*, a true product of science and technology and therefore a perfectly suitable component of a contemporary child's upbringing, whereas religion, still thousands of years old even in its most recent manifestations, is nothing but a collection of dusty untruths, punitive and mean-spirited, an insidious engramatic shackle from which he would eventually have to chew his way free. I would—*so I told myself*—have none of its guilt and fear for him.

Such was my aspiration, in the beginning: for him to be without sin.

"Dad?"
"Hmmm?"
"Do you like to draw, sketch, or even just doodle?"

He didn't wait for my response—a blank stare, as usual—before continuing. Instead, he simply inserted the standard infomercial conversational delay, the artificial hiatus designed to disguise the fact that the person on the television is not actually talking to you, *could not possibly be addressing you personally.*

"If so," he went on, "then you might have what it takes to embark on an exciting career as an artist, illustrator or even draftsman."

These are the times when I most wish his mother were here. So that maybe, just once, his mania would get the attention it deserves. *Gee, I don't know,* she would say. *I've always loved to draw—you know, horses and hot air balloons . . . and I can do an elephant seen from behind in ten seconds flat—but do you really think that means I could be an artist?*

They would go on and on, taking it to the point of absurdity, before finally breaking down in laughter. I would shake my head in mock chagrin, then laugh too.

Instead there is just the silence that marks our being-together. The questions that aren't really looking for answers, the hollow gestures that try to be those answers anyway. We sit stranded on either side of the table, on either side of a bottomless divide between the impersonal and the impossible.

Like that between the television and its audience.

I looked up at him briefly, smiling weakly, then drowned an overcooked broccoli tree in the thick orange lake of melted cheese languishing in the upper half of the Dip-Mor double boiler.

It had been some time since I'd bought a *fantastic modern-convenience device,* since I'd succumbed to one of his parroted sales pitches. Perhaps it was the timing, some beatific resonance generated by the act of tucking him into bed, that weakened me, made me vulnerable.

"Dad?"

The head on the pillow, the only part of him not tucked safely under the covers, seemed so small, the voice so far away.

"Yeah?"

"Did you know that with the Dip-Mor double boiler, not only can you make mouth-watering, chocolate-covered confections, you can also whip up delicious, piping-hot dipping sauces and savory fondues in next to nothing?"

I furrowed my brow thoughtfully, then nodded in agreement, as if the implacable logic of his offer left me no other choice. He smiled and closed his eyes. The next morning, thanks to the miracle of overnight delivery, a shiny new Dip-Mor double boiler—along with instructional video, recipe booklet, four bars of chocolate, dipping tongs and plastic fondue forks—was sitting on our doorstep.

Not that he showed the least bit of interest in it. The first week, I dipped everything I could find in chocolate, tried every sauce recipe in the booklet, made four quarts of fondue, always solo. To be honest, he never acknowledges the presence of any of the products he's sold me. It's as if his share in the matter ends as soon as I give my credit card number to some anonymous late-night operator.

At least the Dip-Mor double boiler has actually proven useful, *usable*, unlike all the other things I've fallen for—the Infinite Lint Roller, the Twenty-Tools-In-One hand drill, the Jerusalem Juicer, the Smoke House 2000, the Magnetron Home Masseuse, the pair of Pocket Fisherman—every one of them back in the box, stacked in the spare closet behind the vintage overcoats and homemade hats and once-fashionable party dresses.

~

Early on I had theories—they were more like *positions*, really—that allowed me to defend or explain away certain discrepancies between the trajectory of *his* education and those of the other little kids at the park.

When it turned out that none of the other four-year olds watched two hours of *Teletubbies* a day, for example. Immediately, the cabal of mothers closed in around me, interrogating.

Teletubbies? Are you kidding? Those little colored . . . things? God, they're creepy! And the show is sooo *dumb, I can't stand it! I mean, sure, maybe it's fine for twenty-four to thirty-six months, but a four-year old? You watch it with him, at least?*

It was like I was feeding him carcinogens, or devolving his DNA. I didn't mention that my son was actually five, or that the show was British.

I sat up on the park bench, pulling my hands from my pockets as I did so, making as if to leave. But for some reason, instead of leaving I said, "It makes sense that you don't get the show. It's not for you. It's a modern folk tale, basically, and it's for the kids, not for us. As far as the Teletubbies are concerned, we're already a lost cause." Not quite sure of where I was going, and therefore unprepared for possible objections, I hurried on. "You see, *Teletubbies* performs a purely didactic function, similar, say, to that of the Grimm Brothers' fairy tales, just for a post-capitalist audience."

I scanned the ring of faces, calculating, based on a quick tabulation of open mouths and blank expressions, the window of time left for whatever it was I was doing.

"Recall your Grimm's," I said. "*The Mouse, the Bird, and the Sausage*, for example. At the outset of the tale, Mouse, Bird and Sausage live a happy, simple life together, as we must assume has been the case since time immemorial. This happiness is dependent on the faithful performance of a clearly defined role: Bird gathers wood for the fire, which Mouse tends, in addition to drawing water and setting the table. Sausage handles the cooking, going so far in the performance of his duties as to use himself to stir and flavor the broth. One day, while out collecting wood, Bird runs into another bird, who tells him that, as he's doing all the hard work in his arrangement with Mouse and Sausage, he's getting the short end of the stick. Bird returns home and demands the three of them swap duties. Sure enough, they're all dead by the end of the next day, Sausage eaten by a dog, Mouse boiled alive in the pot, and Bird drowned at the bottom of a well."

The faces around me, though beginning to show traces of suspicion and impromptu allergies, told me I probably had just enough time to wrap things up.

"I know," I continued sympathetically. "Another story that doesn't make sense. That's because it's not for us, either. It was for 19TH Century German kids. It instructed them, subconsciously, that if you happened to be a bird—i.e. a poor, worthless peasant—nothing good would come of coveting the role, ordained by God and Nature, of a mouse or sausage—i.e. a craftsman or burgher. It also warned these little German kids about the dangers of radicals and outside agitators, told them that only bad things happen when you listen to those who question the natural order of things."

Mouths were now tightly screwed, jaws set, day packs testily prepared for departure.

"Well," I continued, perhaps rushing it a bit, "*Teletubbies* is doing the same thing for our kids, conditioning them to the world they live in, preparing them for the world to come; you know, the world they'll inhabit when they've grown up. In the near future, you see, devices for accepting one-way transmissions from the global communications network will be implanted directly into the human body. And most satisfactions will be virtual and informational, so there won't be much need for gender distinctions. Exposure to *Teletubbies* is therefore essential, since it will help them recognize and accept this future when it engulfs them, even partake of it happily."

Not long after, we stopped going to the yellow park and went to the purple park instead. Following our exile from the purple park, we started hanging out in the plaza, eating our lunch on a weathered, gum-pickled bench and playing tag in the dusty fountain.

These days, we spend most of our time at home, inside.

The nice thing about a double boiler—especially the Dip-Mor, with it's patented NoStik surface—is there's really no way to burn anything. This makes for easy cleanup. No soaking, no scrubbing. So far, the only dilemma posed by the Dip-Mor has turned out to be what to do with all the unused melted cheese.

Standing in front of the kitchen sink, I tilt the upper chamber about forty-five degrees. The cheese lake, now possessed of completely indeterminate properties—it occupies a state somewhere between the liquid and the solid—slides slowly out of the pan, falling in a single quivering piece to the sink before slithering, seemingly of its own volition, down the drain. It's easy to imagine this cheese creature making its way calmly through a labyrinthine network of plumbing and sewage pipes before emerging, silently and under cover of darkness, in some industrial estuary and floating off to sea.

I rinse the inside of the Dip-Mor and set it upside/down on the counter to dry. From the small kitchen I can see into the living room, where he's lying on his stomach in front of the TV, his chin resting in his hands, his legs bent up from the knees, feet waving aimlessly in the air. He's in his pajamas, which I now see are thin and faded, and probably two sizes too small. The TV, I know, is too loud, his face too close to the screen.

This is what it's like, accusations of failure inscribed everywhere.

As always, the feeling comes at me from all sides, an uncanny yet familiar heaviness, like when you're reclining in the dentist's chair and they lay the lead apron over you. And strangely enough, this weight, far from keeping me more firmly anchored to my customary bodily inertia, seems to encourage floating. I leave my body and drift into the living room, the better to watch him slip further away.

Amaze your friends, the TV's saying. I wonder what this phrase could possibly mean to him. *With the incredible Blow d'Art, you can create your very own original works of art. Fantastic creatures, brilliant landscapes, your own Noah's Ark!*

On the screen a little boy, seated at big wooden table, is blowing colored powder at a dinosaur stencil sitting on top of a sheet of craft paper. Blow d'Art. It's the same technology, basically, they used to make the cave paintings. The boy's sister, seated next to him, is putting the finishing touches on a "free hand" rainbow, her eyes maniacal in anticipation of the impending satisfaction. Their mother's face beams down from above.

. . . you get the carrying case, the set of eight One-Way blow tubes, twelve packets of Blow and the complete stencil library. It goes on and on, relentless. They've bought a full minute of airtime. *But that's not all. If you order now, you'll also get . . .*

He's tucked tightly into bed, the blankets wedged beneath his chin, the way he likes. His head is once again small and distant on the pillow. He didn't seem to mind my taking so much longer than usual, didn't seem to notice that I was stalling. I hadn't yet devised a refutation for the Blow d'Art.

"Dad?"

Here we go.

"Hmmm?"

"Did you know that you can also make . . . that with the Dip-Mor double boiler you can also make caramel apples?"

I turn my face to him. I know that this time it shows honest surprise, heartfelt interest. "You know, I never thought of that?"

"Yeah I know. We should make some. Good idea?"

"Yeah. Yeah it is." For once, I think he sees my real face, hears my real voice. I reach out, just like that, and palm the top of his head, tussling his wavy brown hair.

"It's a great idea."

The contact is too much. Already, his smile has faded, replaced by a near absence of expression. And already, my own thoughts begin to wander.

I find myself thinking about the worn, too-small pajamas, stretched tightly over him like a second skin. For some reason, this thought calls to mind the fate of the Grimm's Sausage. In the tale Bird, filled with remorse when Sausage fails to return from his new woodgathering responsibilities, sets off in search of his plump, savory companion. Eventually, he comes across the dog that had so recently devoured his unfortunate comrade. In response to Bird's overwrought accusations of injustice, the dog calmly justified his actions by pointing out that Sausage had been carrying forged papers at the time of their encounter and therefore deserved to die. I have never been able to figure out what this could possibly mean.

sulu

> *This includes the ultimate sacrifice and demonstration of faith—that is, the shedding of your human body. If you should choose to do this, logistically it is preferred that you make this exit somewhere in the area of the West or Southwest of the United States.*
>
> "Exit Press Release" Heaven's Gate® Web Site

WHETHER OR NOT I'M CASTRATED. Ultimately, that was the only question on the minds of job interviewers. I suppose it's understandable. That we had all castrated ourselves is the myth that most persists in the public imagination. Tedious container lovers. They always began to lose interest when I told them I'm still intact. By the time I mentioned that, *as a matter of fact,* only a handful of us were shorn, they'd already marked my application: *Unsuitable for Employment.*

Pi was, though. Castrated, that is; he was the first. So naturally, certain others were going to follow suit. Moonpie, Francis 7, Tron. I remember how the three of them giggled after it was done. Even then it struck me that there was something more going on than mere container evacuation readiness. For my part, I had serious reservations about such actions. I mean, it wasn't clear to me that there was much point in modifying a container you were going to shed anyway.

Which is not to say that I required Pi's doctrine to be logically consistent. Indeed, its telltale incoherence was undoubtedly intentional, a function of his conviction that there are only half-truths; or, that the truth can only be half communicated. He called it "speaking in tongues" and it was the first lesson you learned upon joining the crew. It meant that most of what Pi said could only be understood within the context of protective quotes, a strategy he felt offered the only effective means of cutting through the haze of Luciferian programming that enslaves the mammalian mind. It also explains why, for example, he never felt it necessary to reconcile his fondness for quoting scripture—at least the parts attributed to Jesus—with his otherwise absolute disdain for human religions.

But appearances—the androgyny was easy enough to achieve—and Pi's faith in me aside, I was not a model follower. I had my doubts, to be sure, but I kept my skepticism to myself. Even so, it would be wrong to assume that I wouldn't have joined the group evacuation. It's just that Pi had other plans for me.

~

It's easier, out here, to imagine yourself on the barren, airless face of an alien world than it is to accept that you are still glued to the surface of the earth; that less than fifty miles away human beings dutifully ply the myriad circuits their flesh prisons have compelled them to construct. Regulated traffic patterns. Production/distribution/consumption loops. Diurnal work cycles. Ring-shaped breakfast cereals.

Not that it could be otherwise, given the biological nature of the human vehicular substrate. It's a kind of tragedy—as Pi never tired of pointing out—that humanity so zealously constrains itself to the Human Evolutionary Level, to the shortcomings of the organic container; shortcomings that were, to his mind, invariably cyclical. *What is the human?* he would ask rhetorically. The answer was always the same: an evolutionary zero point. An enzymatic thermostat. Base. Organic.

But I was speaking of my evacuation site, of its unearthly beauty. Unscattered light illuminates the early evening sky, a cosmic background running from blue-gold in the west to violet-black in the distant east. A ceiling of cirrus glows with the hues of a Jovian palette, yellow-pink-lilac-purple, the desert floor smolders pinkish orange. The crimson crown of the sun plunges below the far-off horizon, while a silver moon already cruises at 30°. The intense heat of day has all but dissipated from the valley floor, and a chill night air falls upon the desert. I imagine the cold to be near absolute, myself a being of light impervious to it.

"It's not a punishment, Sulu. It's an honor, in fact. That's how you should think of it. As a responsibility and an honor."

Pi looked at me fixedly with his big, saucer-shaped eyes. I returned his gaze as best I could, searching its depths for some sign of dissimulation. As always, there was only sincerity, bottomless and without emotion, save for a faint glimmer of sadness, an echo of something irretrievably lost. Aside from this tiny chink in its armored surface, Pi's belief was total, so complete it wasn't even a question of belief, really.

It was one week after the discovery of the Bates-Scribner comet. The date for container evacuation had already been set. We sat facing each other on the plush purple carpet of The Porphyry, a small, windowless room attached to the master suite, completely devoid of furnishings, the walls and ceiling painted to match the carpet. It served mostly as Pi's personal prayer chamber, but it was also used as a private backdrop for conversations that could not be conducted according to Minimal Necessary Response ("yes", "no", "I don't know"), the only system of verbal communication allowed in the ship's hallways, sleeping quarters and common spaces.

Our containers were positioned as far apart as the quiet tones of our conversation would allow. Pi had just informed me of his decision: I was to stay behind, to proctor the evacuation, after which I was to continue his work and assemble a crew of my own.

"Of all our once-human plants, you have grown tallest, Sulu. To have awakened and developed your soul to such a degree, in just one period of visitation," he said, his head wagging faintly, "it's no small accomplishment."

I detected the slightest hint of pride in his voice. I too felt a little bit of pride, a filial and banal emotion, of course, but managed not to let it show. I studied the carpet in front of me vacantly.

"And to think," Pi continued wistfully, wondering aloud to himself more than anything. "Your chip would've been the last deposited by the crew that departed this planet just minutes before my own arrival and insertion into this . . ." he gestured with both hands at his seated self, ". . . container."

Pi was referring to Next Level minutes, a Next Level minute being the equivalent of 2.7 earth years. He was fond of remarking on this "coincidental insertion" (he into his body, a recognition chip into mine), never failing to bring it up whenever we had reason to make use of The Porphyry. By Pi's reckoning, a Next Level crew had been here in 1971, tagging my container, five years after its birth, with a recognition chip—the embryo of what humans call a soul—rendering me identifiable to any Beyond Organics subsequently slated to visit the planet on a teaching mission, or "period of visitation." Once identified by a Beyond Organic, I would be offered the opportunity to undergo education and training, during which I would systematically unlearn my organic limitations, gradually sloughing off my human skin until such time as I was ready to disconnect from my container and move to the Next Level.

The anonymous, disembodied voice, a feminine composite, summons the crowd milling about the Arcade: *Lastday, Capricorn 15's. Year of the City: 2274. Carousel begins.* The Logan's Run dream. Renewal. We enter Carousel through doors set in the perimeter of the arena floor. Like the others, I wear a hooded, white silk robe and a white mask. We proceed solemnly, single file, taking our places around a giant red life clock. The increasingly animated spectators spur us on: "Renew! Renew!" We shed our robes, revealing white and red body suits, and begin to levitate, rising from the arena floor toward the shadows far above. The ceremony is not without a certain tension: those of us who drift highest stand the best chance of renewal. I look at the figure closest to me, head thrown back, palms out, life clock blinking red. The figure sparks, then explodes in a burst of flame . . .

I awaken with a start, shivering.

A drop of ice cold water splashes on my forehead. The dark inside my small tent is impenetrable. I pull my arms free of the sleeping bag and activate the IndiGlo backlight on my Casio: 3:40 A.M. And bitterly cold. *So much for my photonic self.* Although I can't see it, I know my breath is steaming, rising and collecting on the tent's inner lining. Still lying on my back, I reach up into the black. My fingertips brush against the nylon fabric and are instantly slicked with moisture. A few more drops shake loose and splash on my face. I take a moment to steel myself, then draw in a deep breath and scramble blindly from the relative warmth of my GoreTex cocoon. Wrapping my still shivering container in whatever clothing I can lay my hands on, I leave the tent and go out into the frigid desert night.

The fire I had built earlier is extinct, its charred skeleton silent. I sit on a large flat rock not far from the tent—hugging my container for warmth—and let my mind drift. The stars are out in numbers that exceed comprehension. Looking up into the sublime expanse, I wonder whether, maybe, my crew mates are actually up there somewhere, trekking happily from one shimmering Next Level star to another.

Not for the first time, my container's throat tightens, and I realize, with a slight tinge of embarrassment, how much I miss the rest of the crew. I had lived with many of them for nineteen years, virtually all of my so-called *adult life*. The last eight years, the ones spent on the ship, were the happiest of my life.

We had accumulated—thanks in large part to timely inheritances—sufficient funds to acquire a suitable "training ship," a two-acre, ten-room estate in a gated subdivision of Rancho Del Viajero. More importantly, we had finally assembled what Pi considered a full complement of crew and no longer had to go on recruiting trips, which always made me feel like a cult member. We were free instead to focus our energy on completing our education, fine-tuning our non-humanness and readying ourselves for the ever-impending container evacuation.

As a further sign of the approach of this event, we closed all channels of communication with the outside world except for those deemed absolutely necessary: the web site design business that was our main source of income, and our own site, from which we continued to broadcast our message, for the benefit of any human plants that might have been tagged but whose germination was not yet complete.

Of ship life, I miss the communal activities most. Pizza and *Next Generation* on Sunday nights, pizza and *Deep Space 9* on Wednesday nights, veggie pot pies and *Babylon 5* on Thursday nights. The annual trips to Sea World to commune with our more highly evolved marine cousins. The Penn & Teller show at the Stratosphere Hotel on the 30th anniversary of Pi's incarnation.

We hardly spoke (outside the confines of Minimal Necessary Response anyway), we never touched, we were all trying to become someone—*something*—different. We were not a surrogate family. We were crew mates. They've been gone for two years now, gone for good—however you choose to look at it—and I do miss them.

~

I looked up at Pi, who was still regarding me with his customary near-blank stare. "You won't be left to do this alone, Sulu. Kirok has been instructed to stay behind and assist you in this task."

Kirok. Out of the entire crew, Kirok was the only real fan of *The Original Series*. But he was more than just a fan. He was a mindless database, a walking factoid, his most original thoughts little more than ill-conceived *TOS* paraphrases. He wore tattered foam-rubber Spock ears to pizza nights. I couldn't stand him. It was Kirok, upon first taking note of my half-Asian descent and slightly pockmarked face, who blurted out the moniker by which I came to be known by the crew. Still, I could understand why Pi chose to leave him behind. Kirok would follow Pi's instructions to the letter (provided he first wrote them down), should I prove unequal to the task.

I couldn't fully disguise my annoyance. Misreading my disquiet for doubt, Pi was quick to offer reassurance. "You know, Sulu, it's only because of my great confidence in you that I entrust the mission to you. The success of our evacuation, and the continuation of our work here on earth, is entirely in your hands."

There was no point in debating the matter. It was already settled. Kirok and I were staying behind. Slowly, I let out my breath, resigning myself to it.

"We will still dine with the away teams, at least?"

"No. I'm sorry. There's much work to be done while we're out. Besides, we're already exceeding the function room's maximum occupancy with thirty. You and Kirok can go after the transport. You should have no problem getting a table for two on a Monday."

I rubbed my eyes. I thought I might come clean right there, but somehow I managed to maintain my dutiful-crewman persona. "Very well."

Pi tilted his head then and gave me his eye-smile. "Don't worry. A ship from Next Level will be dispatched for you and Kirok as soon as I've arrived home."

I almost laughed, despite myself. That was Pi, always shoring things up after the fact.

"How will I recognize it?" I asked, seemingly earnest, playing Sulu, for his benefit, to the end.

"How did you recognize me for what I am? How did you know to come forward and embrace your true nature? How have you managed to transform yourself so completely in such a short period of time? No. It will be obvious, Sulu. It's your destiny."

Pi rose then and made to leave The Porphyry, presumably to gather the other Away Team members for their ceremonial last supper at the nearby Tex-Mex.

I decided not to disagree with him or question him further. His head was filled, as it should have been, with thoughts of destiny. Soon enough—a matter of hours—he and twenty nine others would be meeting it.

I let him go. The time to tell him the truth had long since passed.

Like the Last Man, my heat signature a lone warble of infrared in a cold, dead landscape, I sit and watch the sunrise, touching my lips tentatively to a steaming mug of lemon

TheraFlu. My container converses with itself of its own accord, as usual. *Like the Last Man*, it says. *The rosy fingered dawn*, it says.

The dawn. Another ambiguity. For ages, it has been thought to herald the advent of a new day, a fateful turn in the course of events, the auspicious beginning of a journey. But it symbolizes just as well the never-ending cycle, the Newtonian prison, the lone fact that lies at the bottom of it all: that one is still here, that one is still who one is.

What do I believe? What *did* I believe? It's a difficult question. First, you have to know what Pi believed.

Pi—the spirit-mind-soul-entity that inhabited a container of the same name—claimed to be an emissary from the Next Level Beyond Organic, an advanced "race" of beneficent, pan-galactic beings. In addition to engaging in activities of incommunicable sublimity on their distant home world (the specific details of which Pi never divulged), Beyond Organics comb the galaxy in search of "gardens to seed": worlds and systems where conditions seem amenable to the incubation and development of intelligent life. Indeed, according to Pi it was an older group of Beyond Organics (his grandparents, if I understood him correctly) who first set the ingredients of our own planet's primordial soup to boil.

Earth, then, has been visited frequently by Beyond Organic emissaries, mostly undercover missions undertaken primarily for the purpose of monitoring the development of intelligent life, especially through its fitful preliminary stages (reptilian, mammalian, etc.). Beyond Organics do not permit themselves to interfere with the course of that development, apart from *ensoulment*, the placement of recognition chips. Only in times of dire crisis do Beyond Organics betray their presence and announce their intentions. Indeed, there have been only three such overt missions: that of Prometheus, that of Jesus, and that of Pi himself.

Why, it might be asked, are all beings at Human Evolutionary Level not fitted with recognition chips? The answer, naturally, is that the universe is rife with evil space aliens. Without exception, these aliens are less principled than Beyond Organics. Unlike Pi and his kind, they have no qualms over interfering with the natural development of intelligent life, and seek only to raid the crops on various Beyond Organic garden worlds for their own nefarious purposes.

Such, according to Pi, are the Luciferians, a High Organic Level species from M17 (galactic cluster), by whose agency the development of intelligent life on earth has been permanently arrested. This end was achieved first through the introduction of the concept of the circle into early human culture, then through the implementation of successively elaborate prisons for the Human Level mind: the various religions, with their wheels of fate and reincarnations, their messianic periodicities; a preoccupation with reproduction and its attendant carnality; Newtonian physics; orbital satellites; the global economy; obsessive-compulsive behavior. The sole purpose of this prison system is to provide the Luciferians with a steady supply of "suits." It is this process of turning containers into suits that renders them unsuitable for recruitment to the Next Level.

There can be no escape for the mammalian mind once it has fixed itself on the circle. There was, Pi said, no hope for terrestrial beings at the Human Evolutionary Level. The garden on earth was to be turned over. So he was sent to cultivate as many plants as he could prior to the planet's total destruction. In 1971, Pi incarnated into the container of Morris Appleton, a thirty five year old plant lying in a windowless room in a Galveston clinic, undergoing a cure for homosexuality. After promptly removing himself from the clinic, Pi roamed the southwest, gathering to himself a crew of ensouled containers and preparing them for the impending arrival of a spacecraft, which was to be cloaked in the tail of a short period comet. This craft would return them to the Next Level Beyond Organic.

That, in a nutshell, is what Pi believed.

The evacuation was over almost before it began.

While the Away Teams were at the restaurant, Kirok and I got things ready. I went to the galley and prepared the evacuation agent, an eyedropperful of Phenobarbital mixed in a small cup of chocolate pudding, with an additional squirt dissolved in a shot of vodka for insurance. I prepared thirty of these lethal philters, then loaded them onto a couple of serving trays and carried them up to the evacuation chambers, where Kirok had meticulously arranged a purple silk shroud, a white plate and a new pair of Nike *Decades* on each mattress. I set a serving of pudding and a clear plastic spoon on each plate, along with a paper cup containing the vodka, then went to the Porphyry, where I set up an evacuation kit for Pi. The preparation complete, we retired to our cabins and waited for the others to return.

It was just after eight o'clock when the Away Teams got back from the Tex-Mex. They looked truly impressive in their new black uniforms and freshly cropped hair, like people with a purpose, sexless faces flush with expectation and the efforts of their containers to metabolize their identical last meals: chicken fajitas, fried calamari and a blended margarita (it was essential, according to Pi, that the container be completely sated prior to evacuation).

Any sort of farewell address from Pi—an inspirational toast or speech or a few last words concerning the journey ahead—must have been made at the restaurant. Up to the very moment of their departure, none of the Away Team members said a word.

The teams divided up and went to their respective chambers. Pi, Kirok and I went with Away Team II—comprised mostly of newer crew members and those whose education was not quite complete—to provide a calming presence, just in case. The evacuation agents were consumed silently. There was nothing communal about it. Kirok collected the spoons and empty cups and left the chamber. One by one, the members of Away Team II—Dyson, Klath, Sol, DV8, Tau, Nert, Hrrothy, Qgorn, Odo, Quark, Delorean, THX, Brothos, Laze, Fridge—lay back on their bunks, resting their heads softly on their pillows, and placed the purple shrouds over their faces.

Pi stood in the center of the room, hands clasped behind his back, saying nothing. He did not smile or even blink.

We moved to the room containing Away Team I, a number of whom were original crew members. Even so, things went less smoothly than with Team II. I had known these faces for years. Now, many of them projected doubt, even fear.

I walked over to Francis 7, who had already spooned his cup of pudding clean, only to find himself unable to drain the little paper cup, still sitting on the plate in front of him. He looked up at me and clutched my elbow. I couldn't remember him ever touching another container in the nineteen years I had known him. He looked into my eyes and whispered, "I don't know, Sulu . . . I don't know."

I looked at him with as much compassion as I could muster, pretending that I didn't know either. "I don't know," Francis 7 continued, his voice nearly inaudible, "if it's really going to be there. But I can't stay here any more, I know that. I'm tired of waiting."

I smiled weakly and nodded reassuringly. He looked up at me a moment longer, his eyes darting rapidly from side to side, as if unable to fix on one of mine. I shifted my gaze meaningfully to the little cup. He stared at my forehead for a moment, then seemed to understand. With a heavy sigh, he let go of my arm and picked up the cup. He closed his eyes and threw back the contents with a jerk of his hand, coughing and snorting slightly as he swallowed hard against the innate will to persist. Then he too lay back, retreating beneath his shroud, shutting out whatever light remained to him.

Once again, Kirok cleared away the things. I looked around the room. Pi, apparently, had already left for the Porphyry. Apart from the bodies lying in their bunks, I was alone.

I could feel the foundations of a carefully constructed world coming apart. I could no longer deny—could no longer *pretend* to deny—that we were not really a crew, that we were not really aboard a star ship, that there is no Next Level Beyond Anything. We were simply a crew of lost souls, cohabiting the numb, dreamlike space of a shared hallucination. A hallucination that had been strong enough to transform a sprawling hacienda-style house into a star ship, strong enough for me to assist in the suicide of thirty human beings.

The world, the illusion, in which I had been living was indeed the work of a group. And just like that, the collective desire necessary to sustain it had dissolved, evacuated. Even as the last of my crewmates' shrouds ceased fluttering to their diminishing breath, the lifeblood of fantasy drained from this world, staining everything with its residue. Bodies, beds, rooms, carpets, my very thoughts. It was time to leave the ship.

Taking in the desert landscape languishing beneath the unforgiving midday sun, my container says: *Forbidden Zone*. I am forced to agree with this assessment, forced to recognize the truth of myself in a spontaneous association, in the autonomous chemical engine of memory.

Planet of the Apes. Soylent Green. Rollerball. Logan's Run. Zardoz. These films formed the basis of a personal religion. During my childhood, played out in the days of pre-cable, pre-VCR programming, I missed no opportunity to partake of these escapist sacraments. And there was one common element in these films that captivated me above all else: the presentation of a future.

You see, even at that young age, I was already tired of being here, already tired of earthly things. My innermost desire was to be somewhere else, somewhere different. I took solace in these films, pinning my hopes on the future, on the idea of some place possessing a novel configuration of human existence. It seemed natural to me that such a place could only exist in another time, a future time. The specific features of this future—utopia, dystopia, machine-dominated technocracy, overpopulated nightmare—didn't really matter. What mattered was the chronotope: my belief that, someday, the time of this place would come to pass.

Gradually, this place-to-come became more real to me than the present. I neutralized my predicament through the creation of a fable: my sojourn in the present, I told myself, was a form of exile, a prison from which only the future could deliver me. I kept this fable to myself, layered my life around it, waited.

I shuffled sullenly through adolescence. By the time I reached young adulthood, I was pretty much inert. Time passed, I waited. But my dreamt-of futures never arrived, their projected dates passing by without any of their promises having been realized. No domed cities with their controlled climates and pod cars, no Lucite furniture, no nihilistic spectacles, no soul-crushing totalitarianisms, not even so much as a futuristic typeface.

I had misunderstood time. More specifically, I had misunderstood History, which turns out to be more like spilled milk on a table top. It spreads—call this *progress*, if you want—it expands and changes shape, it thins out some, but ultimately it's still just milk, still white uniformity.

I was just a kid. How could I have known that the future was complicit with the amoebic continuity that is history, that history has no function beyond the inexorable absorption of the potentially alien in its milky sameness?

I was one year out of high school when I came across a flyer for what was obviously a UFO cult. They were looking for people to join the crew of their star ship, people ready to discard their humanness, people willing to journey to a place beyond human.

Bouncing along on the balls of his feet, Kirok intercepted me in the hallway. He had just completed his inspection of the evacuation chambers. As always, he spoke in the choppy, diaphragmatic exhalations of the Shatnerian imperative. "It is done. The transport, it would seem, has been completed successfully."

I wanted to tell him, just so he'd know, how much the rest of us couldn't stand him, how Pi had really left him behind because he couldn't bear the thought of being on the same spacecraft with him for the long journey home.

Kirok would have deferred to me, of course, had I felt like according myself the "honor" of the final inspection. Of the many traits shared by the crew, a love of order and tidiness was foremost. Even after container evacuation, things had to be just right: shrouds smoothed out and properly aligned; arms positioned flush against the sides; fingers uncurled; containers made to looked relaxed and at peace; a roll of quarters in every pocket.

But the attenuated perception required to perceive our world was already lost to me. I knew that, were I were to go back into those rooms, I would not see—as Kirok undoubtedly had—the hallmarks of a "successful evacuation," but rather ordinary suburban bedrooms with rust-colored carpets and tacky window treatments and juvenile bunk beds, all of them made up exactly the same, a uniformed corpse cooling on each mattress.

Unable to summon the energy necessary to communicate with him, I nodded impatiently to Kirok. He frowned at me for a moment, confused, then went off to watch TV. He seemed to have no idea of what was about to happen. Word would get out soon enough: thirty members of a UFO cult had committed mass suicide. The media onslaught would be unparalleled. The cul-de-sac would be choked with throngs of the curious, the righteous, the lonely who wished they could have been a part of it. There would be the families that we had all walked away from—parents, husbands, wives, children—and their lawyers. Possibly, Kirok and I would face criminal charges.

I went straight to the cargo bay . . . I went straight to the garage and climbed up to the rafters, where, among other things, thirty two cardboard boxes were neatly stacked, eight wide and four high. These boxes contained our so-called possessions, whatever things we happened to have with us when we signed on to the crew. A box for each of our pasts. I located mine and pulled it from the stack.

There wasn't much inside. A few LPs, a short stack of science fiction paperbacks, the clothes I was wearing on my arrival—a lavender polo shirt, a pair of acid wash jeans, a black Member's Only windbreaker, some high top Reebok sneakers with a basketball-shaped pump in the tongue. On the bottom of the box sat a blue nylon wallet with a Velcro fastener.

I took the wallet from the box and sat back on the plywood platform, my legs crossed. I tore open the Velcro seal. The telltale sound of that tear was like a hypnotist's recall phrase. The weight, the false reality, of the past nineteen years cracked, falling away like the husk of a chrysalis, only to reveal that I was still a worm. I examined the driver's license tucked behind the clear plastic panel. I read the name. Bruce Nomura.

There was a faint ringing in my ears. I gazed numbly at the strangely familiar countenance staring back at me from the photograph. It had my eyes, but the face was rounder, fuller. The hair was long, not close-cropped, it fell almost to the shoulder. And it was smiling, this face. The woman had told me to smile, so I did. I. Me. Bruce Nomura. The one I didn't have it in me to be the first time. The one, thanks to the untimely appearance of the Bates-Scribner comet, I would have to become again.

There were eighty dollars in the zippered bill compartment. I went through the rest of the boxes then, taking any cash I found. There was enough to last a week or so. I changed into my old clothes. Apart from the sneakers, they were actually a little big and, I suspected, probably out of fashion. Not that it mattered. I left my loose fitting Next Level uniform in the box.

I thought about taking one of the *Next Level Web Design* vans, then decided against it. That would only give them something to search for. Instead, I simply opened the garage door and set off down the street.

I was about twenty yards from the house when I heard the front door open. Still walking, I looked back over my shoulder. Kirok was standing on the front porch, his right arm outstretched in a half-waving, half-beckoning gesture. He called out once: "Sulu?"

I left him standing there, his head tilted, mouth hanging open. Three months later, after being duped of the film rights to his story by an unscrupulous journalist, Kirok evacuated his container in a hotel room just outside Long Beach.

It's been two years since I walked away from Rancho del Viajero.

I was no better at being Bruce Nomura the second time around. I gave it my best shot, which admittedly wasn't much. I spent two months working as an entry-level database programmer for a multinational corporate cult, secured a few short-term "web consulting" jobs. I made no friends, of course; you need to be able to look at people, acknowledge their presence, for that. Inevitably, I began to think of my nondescript one bedroom apartment as an escape pod.

I thought of the crew. I thought: *what if?* I liked to tell myself that *maybe* the others had been like me, just science fiction fans who somehow felt more at home in a harmless, consciously chosen, well guarded fantasy. That, like me, they were in it for the pizza nights and the pretense of life on a star ship. But they *were* different. They evacuated. Ultimately, they left because they believed that a better place exists, that they would actually attain this place if only they could make it to the other side of the galaxy. In the end, they needed the future even more than me. Like Francis 7, they had grown tired of waiting for it.

But it's not just thoughts of the crew that have haunted me of late. My container has also grown fond of repeating John 12:25, Pi's favorite bible verse. *He who loves his life will lose it, and he who hates his life in this world will keep it for eternal life.* In other words, it's suicide not to commit suicide. Such was Pi's wager. When you're trapped between two worlds, like me, there's no alternative but to accept it.

I'm not exactly sure what I'm hoping for. Not to mention the issue of how far my evacuation kit strays from the rigorous protocol laid down by Pi. I've got a purple handkerchief for a shroud, generic black sneakers from the HugeMart (the *Decades* were pulled from the shelves practically the day after the evacuation), orange Jell-O and Fanta soda for evacuation agents. There are no comets currently in the neighborhood of earth. I've forgotten the roll of quarters.

Still, poised on the very threshold of evacuation, I, *Sulu*, do feel hope, or at least a sense of relief.

I lay back on my sleeping bag and place the shroud over my face. Inside the tent it's like a sauna. A little bit of light filters through the soft purple fabric. I close my eyes. Under the combined influence of the heat and the evacuation agent, I begin to relax, losing all sense of my container's physical boundaries. It's like a return to the womb. Then . . .

My final thought.

Your container, it would seem, is with you to the end. It says, *This is my final thought.*

I watch.

It's a memory, fuzzy around the edges, but still full of vibrant color. I'm sitting in the back of a non-descript middle class automobile, my face pressed close to the passenger-side window. My mother is dragging me along on some errand or other. We're driving down our town's so-called *main thoroughfare*, in reality little more than a two-lane road divided by a concrete traffic island. A month or two before, the island had been outfitted with an immaculate Astroturf lawn. I immediately recognized the glistening island as a beacon of progress, a promise from the not-too-distant future. It was the only patch of town that I actually liked. My last thought, then, is to relive the moment when I first beheld the death of my private utopia. For already, you see, the uniform blades of plastic grass were infested with cigarette butts and small scraps of paper. And all along the compromised seams of this fleetingly-perfect petrochemical oasis, ugly, prickly weeds were thriving.

neighbor

I SIT CROSS-LEGGED on a braided oval rug, absently working the ragged edges of a crispy scab on my knee with the tip of a humid, pudgy forefinger. A slow-moving stream of rhinoplasm, fallout of an ongoing skirmish between my immune system and some low-grade bacterium, creeps steadily from my left nostril, necessitating periodic sniffing. Otherwise, my entire being is given over to the man on the TV.

The neighbor woman into whose care I am delivered each morning, and who hands me over in turn to the care of the television, maintains only the highest scruples when it comes to the preservation of my faculties of sight and hearing. I have long since learned not to sit within ten feet of the screen, and the volume is never set at a level that might be heard above the the neighbor woman's countless phone conversations—which she invariably dominates—and the ominous clamor of housework, punctuated by the cupboard slammings and dish clatterings that signal her hourly descents into transient bouts of micro-rage.

Naturally, given such conditions, I catch only fleeting and fragmentary snippets of the program's dialogue, the majority of which seem to be concerned with neighbors and neighborhoods and neighborliness and being a neighbor.

No matter. It's not the audio portion of the program—a sequence of polite conversations between the soft-spoken man and various puppets and minor civil servants—that captures my attention. The sound, in fact, could just as well be turned off. What fascinates me is the show's *spatial* dimension; that is to say, its set.

For the most part, the set depicts the interior of the man's house, itself set in the midst of a model community. Literally. It's a town in diorama. On a tabletop overlaid with painted streets and parks sit model houses and shops, a model post office and railroad crossing, a model church and fire department. Clusters of model citizens are sprinkled about street corners and storefronts. A red model trolley makes its way through the town's tidy streets and right-angled intersections, eventually passing in front of an archetypally unassuming house. The man's house.

My gaze piggybacks the camera as it inches forward toward the tiny front door. We've gained the front porch, we're poised before the door. Then, at the precise moment when, *in my mind*, I reach out for the knob, the camera cuts to an interior shot centered, one must assume, on the same door, now of normal dimensions.

The door opens and the man enters the house, closing it softly behind him. Having come from outside, he sports a light blue windbreaker, zipped halfway so that it might reveal the powder blue shirt and brown and yellow striped tie beneath. He wears navy slacks and brown, hard-soled shoes.

The man turns and looks at me. He smiles. His narrow face is kind, there's a grandfatherly gleam in his eyes. His lips are red and moist. His hair—light gray at the temples, darker on top—is neatly parted to one side, firm, orderly. The part is so precise as to make it seem as if his hair is actually a combination of two separate but complimentary pieces. It suggests a harmony outside space and time.

The man's lips are moving, but his voice is drowned out by the noise from the vacuum cleaner, which the neighbor woman is hoovering violently down the hall toward the spare bedroom. Still, I can tell he's singing, communicating something friendly to me, something neighborly.

Now the man, having opened the door to the coat closet, is calmly removing his jacket. In a single fluid motion, he takes the zipper pull between his thumb and forefinger, guides it smoothly toward his waist. The teeth slide open, the jacket separates from his body in a controlled fall, the man taking special care that the sleeves do not turn inside/out. Still facing me, still silently smile-singing, the man floats his left hand into the closet. Without the slightest fumble, the hand emerges a moment later with a wooden hanger. The jacket is draped effortlessly on the hanger and admitted to the closet, in exchange for a blue cardigan.

Happily mouthing the words to his song, the man puts on the sweater, becomes one with it. First one sleeve, then the other, there's no hurry, each button married in turn to its corresponding hole. He removes his hard-soled shoes in a similar manner, replacing them with a pair of canvas sneakers. Shoes for the inside.

In my memory of this program, I also see myself watching it. I see my fingertip gradually wedging further beneath the scab. I see myself breathing through a slightly open mouth to compensate for my increasingly clogged nose. I see my eyes darting about, hungry, scouring the screen for every last quantum of possible meaning. I assimilate the lesson without question. That's what it is, a lesson. Why else, after all, would the people responsible for my care place me in front of this program, day after day, if not for the sake of instruction, if not to allow for the imprint of information vital to my future well being and survival?

I pay close attention to the lesson, absorb its intent.

The careful arrangement of things, useful things, in space. A space with things that can be touched, implements that can be handled, utilized, returned to their proper place. A place for everything and everything in its place. The coat in the closet, the arm in the sleeve, the button in the hole. Inside, outside. This is what a house means.

Moving between things. Picking things up, holding them, using them, returning them. The proper employment of hands and fingers. This is what it means to *be in a house*.

Like water in water.

The hand holds the canister of fish food, the finger taps just the right number of flakes into the tank. The spine of the open storybook rests in the palm of the hand, the finger glides along beneath the words on the page. The mouth smiles, the lips are red. The tongue moistens the seal on the flap of the envelope, the finger smooths it closed. The tongue licks the stamp, the thumb and finger affix it to the envelope. This is the information that imprints itself. This is the lesson I absorb. *Why not?* For what other reason would they have placed me in front of the television?

The program nears its end.

The neighbor woman is in the spare bedroom now, the vacuum's predatory roar muffled by the intervening walls. My forefinger has worked the scab loose, it's poised on the tingly threshold of detachment. In a moment it will break free, a rogue continent of scurfy matter. A drop of blood will seep slowly from the spot where it had been anchored, a tiny pinhole in the fresh pink skin. A new scab will begin to form.

In a moment, the neighbor woman will finish vacuuming. She'll step on a button on the machine's cylindrical body, the cord will whip its way violently home, coil up in the dark insides. She'll wrestle meaningfully with the unwieldy appliance, bully it into the closet, then labor, deeply aggrieved, down the hall.

In a moment, her shadow will fall over me, her breath. With alarming peremptoriness, the television will be turned off and she'll usher me to the spare bedroom, where I'll spend the rest of the day in the company of splintered alphabet blocks, a three-wheeled truck, plastic army men.

In the relative quiet of the meantime, I hear the words of the man's farewell song, which I always remember as if they had been whispered: *. . . there's no-body quite so spe-cial . . . as you.*

numb

Late afternoon. The television is on. I lie down on the couch and am soon fast asleep. I have the following dream:

I find myself hovering over a three-story stairwell reminiscent, in its materials, lighting and peculiar sonorities, of those found in public high school buildings of the 1950s. Lacking additional evidence, I am nevertheless aware that the building is in fact a scientific research facility, engaged primarily in work on *genetics*.

A small group of scientists, complete with lab coats and pre-war eye wear, is gathered on the stairwell's second floor landing. Each has come there independently, to bear witness to strange events and share with the others suspicions of supernatural goings-on. None of them, it would seem, question the unlikely coincidence of their arrival.

Being scientists, each of them has been driven to the verge of paranormal confession with the utmost reluctance, and only after the accumulation and analysis of irrefutable evidence. As they all begin speaking at once, it is some time before they realize that each of them is repeating exactly the same utterance. The implication of this fact, that the irrational knowledge they had been forced to accept independently (and the burden of which each thought to shoulder individually) is common knowledge, shared by them all, sinks in even more slowly. Relieved, their personal suspicions having been corroborated in turn by each of their peers, they begin speculating wildly and animatedly, in urgent but hushed tones.

I am not, as of yet, directly involved in the dream's action. My actual self (with its normal point of view, the one with which I perceive the real world) has not been inserted into the oneiric chain of events; nor is there an avatar, some embodiment of myself serving as the privileged locus of my own attention within the unfolding narrative. I no sooner become aware of this non-involvement then I realize that it is in fact my very immanence in the dream, pervasive yet unmanifested, that is the source of the scientists' unease.

It is only then, at the precise moment of this realization, that I find myself (my *self*) drawn into the action. Ceasing to enjoy the perspective of a spectral observer from some impossible beyond, I find myself on the landing among the group of scientists, one of them.

I waste no time in communicating my insider's knowledge, as much to curry favor with senior staff members as from an unmotivated desire to be helpful. I add my self-assured utterances to the chorus of whispers: *There's nothing to worry about. Your reality is in fact a dream, and the source of your fears is just the vague presence within it of me, the Dreamer.* Like them, I repeat my statement, ignoring its apparent ineffectuality. Then, one by one, they cease speaking and turn their attention to me. Not because of the importance of what I'm saying, however, but because of the manner in which my message issues forth. The harsh, scratchy echoes of their purposeful whispers dissipate in the cavernous stairwell, gradually replaced by a truly unearthly sound, like that of a large carcass—upon which a small radio emitting only static has been placed—being dragged across a wet cement floor. This sound is none other than my own speech.

Their looks of authentic irritation over being interrupted by such an inappropriate noise give way to expressions of professionally fascinated disgust. They quickly regain their composure (these are my colleagues, after all), each assuming the bedside manner of a physician for whom informing patients of their terminal status is old hat. But it's too late, I know that something is horribly wrong with me.

And then their faces literally become mirrors, allowing me to see that the inner lining of my left cheek has been overtaken by a parasitic growth, pomegranate red and with the texture and consistency of caviar. Although I know it to be inappropriate, I cannot help but think of the word *spongiform*. Already, this growth has begun to spill out of the corner of my mouth.

My alarm at this turn of events is considerable.

The appearance of this viral mutilation—and my attendant reaction—is accompanied by a sudden influx in the dream of supernatural *presence*, felt even by myself, and the group scatters. I find myself running, with a few others whom I do not recognize, through a long corridor. The low-cut rust-colored carpet and regularly spaced doors with view holes and brass numbers lead me to understand that the building, in addition to being a high school and scientific research facility, is also a motel. I turn abruptly through the door on my left and enter a large anteroom. Two junior staff members, a man and a woman, both quite attractive and sporting contemporary hairstyles and eye wear, are seated at a long folding table, filling out questionnaires. To the right of the table is a set of double doors, leading into an auditorium where some sort of convention—nothing scientific—is being held. The junior staff members shush me simultaneously, even as I spot a rest room off to one side. I burst through the door and rush melodramatically to a mirror, where I confirm what I fear most: the spongy mass spilling out of my mouth is slowly but steadily growing.

The dream then comes to a forced and artificially rapid denouement. It turns out that, while no cure can be found to eradicate the strange growth, it can be cut back painlessly (to a point), much as one would trim a moustache. In fact, standard beard trimming equipment can be easily adapted for this purpose. It is now many years later, and I am standing in front of a bathroom mirror engaged in this very act, which has long since become a normal part of my daily hygienic regimen.

I awaken abruptly. Across the room, my son is calling my name repeatedly. The left side of my face, upon which

I have apparently been sleeping at an odd angle, has gone completely numb.

mother of god

Not prophets only, but neither angels nor archangels have seen God. For how can a creature see what is uncreated.
                                                            - John Chrysostom

I'M RUNNING AS FAST AS I CAN. Admittedly, the pace falls somewhat below my capabilities, but you have to consider the seven pints of Guinness sloshing around my gut and the Virgin clutched tightly to my chest beneath my buttoned-up windbreaker. I'm waddling, basically. It's hard not to waddle when you're running without the use of your arms and your sense of equilibrium has been compromised by a gallon of stout. It's hardly a gait designed for speed, the waddle, what with all the inefficient, side-to-side motion, but I'm giving it an honest effort. It's a brisk waddle.

The segmented sidewalk rises sharply beneath my feet, heaved by the groping roots of a large maple in the adjacent front yard, plate tectonics in miniature forming a kind of ramp from which I launch myself skyward, landing gracelessly a couple of feet later. The sidewalk then dips slightly, following the contoured slope of a driveway entrance. A predictable topographical pattern emerges—the trees, driveways and three-family houses were placed here at the same time, after all—and I settle into a nice, steady, waddling rhythm.

But the cloud of voices behind me sounds closer now, thicker. I find it impossible to believe that the chicken-legged wretches are actually gaining ground on me. At least the ones from *The Shield*; honestly, those people spend their entire waking lives inside that bar. The neighborhood watch people are another story; they could be cops or paramedics for all I know.

I risk a glance over my shoulder. Behind me, the entire street is bathed in a film of weak, powdery light, the color of children's aspirin. *Why, exactly, was the whole world switched over to these disheartening orange street lamps?* I'm leaning toward the theory that it was undertaken solely for the aesthetic enjoyment of airplane passengers when, still gazing behind me, I become mesmerized by my vaporous breath as it trails off into the chill night air, a transient chaos of swirling eddies and vortices. Understandably, I fall out of step with the *predictable topographical pattern*, and trip headlong over a raised slab of buckled concrete.

It's like the fall of a bound man, without hands to break it—mine being, in this instance, still committed to the Virgin. I land hard, coming down directly on top of the statue (or is it *statuette?*), the air from my lungs expelled in a rush as if from a bellows. I skid a few feet before coming to a stop.

Somehow, I manage to keep my head raised during the fall, so my teeth and consciousness are intact. It's from this vantage point, prone, my face about six inches off the ground, that I see the head of the Madonna come tumbling out of my jacket and bounce along the sidewalk like a lumpy roulette ball. It describes a slight leftward arc before tottering over the curb into the gutter.

I want to laugh, I try to; it's hilarious, really. But I haven't the lungs for it. Instead, I roll onto my back, gasping for breath. The sides of my hands sting sharply. Holding them up in front of my face, I can see they're pretty well scraped and already bleeding. This is okay. It's a childhood injury and I welcome it. A different kind of pain registers from my left knee, though, a deep throbbing beneath a burgeoning numbness; a grown-up injury, for sure.

Pulling myself up into a seated position, I can see that my pursuers are now just a little over half a block away. And they've seen me. There are definitely more of them now. It's starting to look like a bona fide rabble. No doubt about it; I underestimated them. Not that it's entirely my fault. Who could have expected motion sensitive lighting, trip wires, *alarmed* grottoes, after only one week?

So much for my master plan.

Taking the now headless statue from my jacket, I toss it over the waist-high chain link fence bordering the nearest yard. It lands on the permafrost lawn with a heavy thud. As a final nod to my misguided sense of superiority, I tell myself that this might somehow slow them down, provide some sort of diversion. Then I retrieve the lump of painted plaster from the gutter and hobble off in search of a suitable hiding place.

~

I don't belong here.

I don't mean this situation; I'll take my share of responsibility for that. I mean this town. I don't belong here. If my life has stood for anything, it's the attempt to transcend places like this. Places like the one where I grew up, places like this one here, where I live now. Not to get above them; it's not an elitist thing. Not entirely. I just want to get beyond them, outside them. *Free* of them. I'm pretty sure the people who live here would agree with me: I don't belong here.

And yet, it's precisely here that I always end up. A never-ending string of heres with a few theres thrown in just to make sure I have cause enough for longing and regret.

There are no special circumstances behind my being here. No high paying job with good prospects for advancement. No pulsating nightlife. No love interest. Nor, as far as I can tell, is there some compulsive tendency, on my part, to self-destructive behavior. I'm not the kind of person who willingly places himself in dangerous situations. I've given it plenty of thought, of course, but I've been able to discern no discrete pathology, no clear-cut intersubjective conflict decided in favor of, say, masochism, that could account for my habitually questionable choice of residence. Indeed, in all other matters, I consider my judgment to be quite sound.

Whatever.

The rent's cheap, the place has hardwood floors; I'm not all that far from the city. During a heavy snowfall, when everything sits under a soft, curvy cushion of snow and visibility is reduced to about twenty feet, my neighborhood can actually look somewhat beautiful.

From a purely physical standpoint, my neighborhood is easily described. Block upon block of three story wooden rectangles, for the most part completely devoid of what traditionally passes for architectural detail or ornamentation.

Built between 1880 and 1910 and descended from the Mansard-style row house (minus the charmingly distinctive roof line), these simple geometric structures were created as part of a conscious effort to afford hard-working, blue-collar immigrant families a means of escaping the over-crowded nightmare of the urban tenement. A family could rent one of the three comparatively roomy flats, or even purchase the building itself, living in one flat and paying the mortgage with the rent from the other two. This humble manifestation of the American Dream was given a suitably modest name: the three-decker.

But nothing is more loathsome to what is than a dream on the verge of reality, especially one that would bring immigrants into the communities of mainstream Americans. So those mainstream Americans grudgingly roused themselves from their gilded narcosis just long enough to crush the upstart dream underfoot. In the guise of "safety reform," they launched the necessary crusades, drafted and passed the appropriate zoning laws, and then returned, their enclaves legally inoculated against the virulence of foreign tongues and swarthy skin, to their own dreams of cozy, eugenicist prosperity.

Within a generation, the unjust circumstances of the neighborhood's stillborn existence were all but forgotten. The houses remained, of course, and were duly bequeathed to sons and daughters, the best of which are now absentee landlords and count themselves among the ranks of the mainstream. The rest merely squat their homes in a state of perpetual near-bewilderment, partners in a proto-suburban *Totentanz*.

At some point in the not so distant past, the mythical king of property improvement salesman blew through town, leaving in his wake entire streets of wrought iron and chain link fence, simulated brickwork, aluminum siding, vinyl windows, asphalt driveways. It's possible that this rococo toupee was consciously donned, intended, perhaps, as an antidote for the otherwise total absence of detail. I think it more likely, however, that the locals simply find solace and protection in the profusion of banal, quasi-sacred objects. As if the bottomless void at the heart of being could be filled with tchatchkies.

Whatever the case, the flood of do-it-yourself home customization has only had the paradoxical effect of intensifying the perception of an underlying absence of substance. It could be that the part of the brain entrusted with taking notice of fanciful detail simply ceases to function in the presence of so many wrought iron curlicues.

The few remaining houses not effectively sheathed in space-age polymers—those, in other words, still clad in the original wood shingles and trim—lie somewhere between garden-variety decrepitude and imminent-condemnation on the Neglect & Disrepair scale.

Yet, despite it all, there exists a strange and pervasive pride of place, which can only strike the outside observer as unfounded and even a little sad. It's called a "code of honor" or something here, but it's more like an agreement of the damned to stick it out to the end, bound by suffering and misery. Maybe it's one of those "human spirit" things of which people are so fond of talking. Whatever it is, it bothers me.

Not that I'm laying blame. We're born into a world built on the twisted remains of crushed dreams. Some people become aware of this fact and some don't. In neither case can the situation be altered. You just feel it here more than elsewhere: a broken dream and reality are the same thing.

Anyway, about a year ago I took a second floor flat in one of these giant shoeboxes. A white woman in her thirties, perfectly resembling a mouse, in her appearance as well as in her approach to life, lives alone on the first floor. Above me, a tight-knit Colombian family of six to eight lives together in what is by far the smallest of the building's three apartments. These are the hardest working people I have ever seen, each holding down several jobs, practically around the clock. The hour is not far off when they will have worked their way to greener pastures.

I long for the day. For it just so happens that the only game their three small children know is running back and forth across the length of the apartment in their hard-soled shoes, at all hours of the night.

But I have a luxurious amount of space for one person: two rooms (a bedroom and another that I like to call "the parlor"), a large kitchen, a freshly renovated bathroom with a quaint, claw foot tub, and decks on the front and rear of the house. I even created a small "study" by removing the double doors from the parlor's spacious closet. As a sort of fortification against the outside world, I lined the wall facing the street with books. A few sturdy, functional pieces of second-hand furniture, a couple of plants and some reproductions of Russian Constructivist posters that I cut out of a book and tacked to the walls round out the décor. For the most part, I keep the shades drawn.

There must be an unwritten law of social organization requiring neighborhoods to have a self-appointed den mother/guardian angel. The incarnation of this archetypal busybody in my neighborhood is Marie Healy, a rambling wreck of a woman, perhaps sixty years old. Marie is composed primarily of an awe-inspiring mantle of sagging flesh, seemingly defenseless against the Earth's gravitational forces. She is typically clothed in a knee-length polyester housecoat, to all appearances converted from a queen-size Days Inn bedspread. She wears the coat virtually 365 days a year, "'cept fah special occasions," having been forced into this unfortunate fashion compromise, she confessed one day, "onaccounta my shingles."

Marie lives in one of the wood shingled "originals," in need of a fresh coat of paint but otherwise in good condition, which she shares with her "baby brotha" Roger, a fifty-year old fireman currently on some sort of disciplinary leave. Marie euphemistically refers to his employment status as an "onrabul dischahj," her right eye blinking strangely whenever she tells me this. I've not yet been able to determine if this blink is meaningful or merely symptomatic of an uncontrollable nervous disorder, so I don't know if her remark was intended ironically or not. It's doubtful. For my part, I suspect his "leave" has something to do inveterate drinking or inveterate racism. Or both.

Marie's house happens to be directly across the street from mine, which is how I came to know that she is also the neighborhood's self-appointed snoop. I had ventured out to collect my mail one afternoon, one of the few occasions when I am completely vulnerable to attack. Marie, sitting saggily on her front porch as usual, pounced immediately, nodding her head in the direction of my front window and blurting out the indictment: "You shure gottalotta books in theh." I smiled weakly at her and waved vaguely, in feigned ignorance of the fact that she had actually spoken to me. She opened her mouth to say something more, but I had already retreated, like a startled crayfish, back into my apartment.

It was in the hopes of fitting quietly into the neighborhood that I tried to take advantage of Marie's compulsive voyeurism, purchasing a pair of colored pencil portraits of Pope John Paul II and John F. Kennedy. I put them in matching frames, then hung them carefully on the wall that served as the terminus of her line of sight.

Two days later, I looked out my window to see her crossing the street with ceremonial officiousness, her ambiguous bulk rendered strangely fluid thanks to an odd, dissimulating effect of her housecoat. In her hands was a turquoise Corning ware bowl with a tinfoil lid. She was heading straight for my house.

The doorbell rang.

I went slowly down the stairs to the front door, opening it about eight safe, significant inches. Marie smiled at me through the gap, awaiting an invitation inside.

I waited back, stone-faced. I had no intention of letting her cross my threshold. As far as I was concerned, she had already seen enough of my apartment.

Though momentarily thrown for a loss in the face of my unexpectedly uncivil attitude, she managed to regain her composure with admirable swiftness. She smiled again, thrusting the bowl through the narrow opening with one arm. I took it from her and set it on the stairs behind me, certain that I did not want to know what was inside, then continued my silent waiting.

"It's ambrozier sallid," she said finally, apparently concerned that I might have failed to fully appreciate the precious nature of her offering.

" 'Food-a-God,' they call it."

"I think it's 'food of *the gods*,'" I replied, wondering why I had opened the door. "God is already a food."

A puzzled look, more of a squint than a frown, fluttered across her face like a malevolent palsy, quickly replaced by the return of her insincere smile. She was here in an official capacity, neighborhood business. She would not be stayed by any unforeseen oddity on my part. At least not until she had performed her duty, after which there would be time enough for judgment and disapproval.

"Well, whatevuh. It's a dessert mostly, but you can eat it whenevuh ya like." She added, in a confessional/conspiratorial tone: "I usually has a little bowl at night, right befah Leno."

She was genuinely happy, I knew, to be able to share this information with me. I was actually somewhat surprised when she failed to strafe me with the details of how her sofa massages her backside while she watches.

"Well, thank you very much, *Mrs . . . ?*"

"Marie. Just Marie. I'm not married."

No kidding? Somehow, I found the strength to resist giving voice to the fatuous compliment we both knew to be customary. Instead, I stared at her evenly for another moment or two.

Then, "Thanks again, Ma-*rie*."

A clearly disappointed squint/smile. "Well, okay then. G'night." She turned to go, then stopped, shooting me a sidelong glance. *Good God*, I thought. *Here it comes: a test.*

"To be honest, I just thank Mary you're not anothawona those ricechoppas."

It was my turn to squint. Then I remembered the name of the family who occupied the flat prior to me. *Nguyen*. It was still dyno-labeled on my mailbox.

"Pahdon the expression." She grinned at me slyly. Eleanor Roosevelt teeth, shallow gums. The mouth of a horse.

I had the appropriate visions right there: I was the terrible instrument of a righteous fury, a white-hot glow reducing her to a smoldering pile of ashes in an instant; I was Old Testament wrath. It wouldn't have taken much, I could've berated this woman with a skeleton crew of neurons, could've done it in my sleep. At the very least, I might have mentioned something about how the former occupants of my apartment had moved to their very own house in a neighborhood that was actually on a par with Holocene standards. And yet, when it came to it, I wasn't even able to produce such an insignificant salvo.

Instead, I said, "Well, the odds were in your favor, considering it's winter."

Her face bunched up completely, like a wet sponge mop drawn in a wringer. "Beg ya pahdon?"

"It's the cold," I explained, matter-of-factly. "It's hard to be calculating and industrious in cold weather. *They* don't like it."

Worn cogs turned ponderously, lights dimming under the strain. I talked funny, but maybe there was some hope for me yet. Then she nodded her head vigorously. I was tempted to reach out in order to steady her quivering cheeks. She beamed at me, smiling openly. I had understood, I had passed her test. I had even given her a new scientific-sounding fact with which to regale her friends when they were finished extolling the dubious virtues of their bunions and carbuncles. *It's the cold, ya see, they don't like it.*

"Ya *name?*" she repeated.

"I don't think I caught yah name, dear."

Dear. So, there it was. My atonement had already begun. I'd lost an opportunity for moral remediation but gained a big, fat, racist aunt. I resolved not to tell her my real name. A pyrrhic victory, to be sure, but she had already sucked enough life-force out of me for one day.

"DeWayne," I said with a twang.

A half squint. "Don?"

"Yeah, sure, that's it. *Don.*"

She reached out then and actually patted my forearm.

"Well, welcome to the neighbahood, Don. Gahbless. And doantchu worry about the bowl. I'll come ovah for it tamara."

I shut the door, close on her heels, afraid that she might succumb to an afterthought and invite me over for some unspeakable casserole. I watched through the highest of the three diamond-shaped panes of glass set diagonally in the door as she returned home, negotiating the tricky descent of my front porch steps with saintly equanimity. The long, cold trek back across the street and up the steps of her own porch proved no less triumphal for her. She walked slowly, solemnly, letting her flame-retardant housecoat fall partially open, as of to indicate that she, for one, was impervious to the cold.

Given the proper equipment, an analysis of the netherwordly air exhausted from the fan above haggard entrance to *The Shield* would yield more knowledge of the human condition/predicament than all the razed libraries of antiquity combined. Indeed, if we really wanted to transmit an accurate representation of Earth culture to an intelligent alien species, it would have sufficed to send *The Shield* itself on an interstellar trajectory, in place of the ludicrously optimistic plaque on the Voyager craft, with all of its irrelevant information on our genetic structure and mathematical aptitude. We'd probably find ourselves under galactic quarantine inside of a light minute.

At the very least, the brief whiff of Venusian atmosphere blasted from the bar's air handler at passersby impresses upon them the fact that dedicated professionals are hard at work inside.

I went because I needed a beer. But not only a beer. The snowless, bitterly cold winter had me depressed. And lonely. I was desperate, I admit, for some form of social contact. Even if it was only to be in my usual quiet-observer/cynical-outsider mode, I needed to be among *people*. I chose *The Shield* simply because it's the only bar within reasonable walking distance of my apartment.

It was almost 10:30 when I opened the door and stepped inside. It's a small place, just big enough to accommodate the usuals, with their chapped, swollen faces and irregular torsos, a bar about a dozen stools long, and three booths, with hard, orange plastic seats and white laminate table tops. The walls, clad in simulated light oak paneling, were otherwise unadorned. A plenum of smoke filled the space between the walls, so thick it didn't so much as swirl when you walked through it. The smoke-tainted, wall-size mirror behind the bar was so overwhelmed with publican effluvia that only a few grainy patches still offered bar goers a glimpse of their somber reflections.

On this particular evening, the bar was fairly crowded, with people tightly clustered along its length in groups of three or four. The crowd thinned out near the far end of the bar, where a few lonely souls were gazing silently at an old Trinitron hanging from the upper corner. On screen, Jimmy Smits was weaving his way on foot through the hazardous streets of an *NYPD Blue* rerun. The harshly lit booths were unoccupied.

I fully expected to be greeted by a sea of hostile, reproachful looks. Instead, only a few heads swiveled expectantly—and somewhat fearfully—in my direction, looking me over long enough to determine that I wasn't a jealous spouse or bookie muscle before swiveling back to their drinks with noticeable relief.

I squeezed my way up to the bar and waited quietly. About two minutes passed before the bartender, a small, wiry man with limp black hair and a thin moustache—a dead ringer for the late Billy Martin—reluctantly acknowledged my presence. He took my order silently, avoiding eye contact, then rifled about behind the bar, muttering under his breath. He returned with something like a pint glass in hand, which he slapped under the slow-pouring Guinness tap before wandering back to his spot beneath the television.

Waiting for my pint, I had no choice but to contemplate the appalling collection of detritus on the back mirror, fixed there as if by some demonic force. Among the more notable *objets perdu*: a Miller Beer poster in which three balloon-breasted swimsuit models were ogling, with clear sexual intent, a sweaty, life-size bottle of The High Life; a handful of humorous bumper stickers (*Yes, As A Matter of Fact I Do Own the Whole Damned Road!* HONK IF YOU LIKE HONKING!! SEXY GRANDMA!!!); obsolete season schedules for the local sports teams; an autographed head shot of Merlin Olsen from his Little House days; a stuffed, moth eaten squirrel, poised for all eternity before the prospect of an unopened acorn; an opaque, white-plastic carousel lamp, around which the Budweiser Clydesdales endlessly cantered; a counterfeit twenty taped next the till, alongside IDs confiscated from a handful of personae non grata.

There was only item from the banal array of cultural jetsam of interest to me, a hand-worked wooden key rack, which doubled as a small diorama of a Mexican Bar. The scene depicted three weary *campesinos* sitting at a bar, in existential isolation from one another, hunched forlornly over their beers. A fourth lay passed out on the floor beneath his wool poncho.

I've always been susceptible to the ineluctable charm of dioramas, especially miniatures. I could already feel myself falling under the spell of the parallel world disclosed by this cheap box of wood, plastic and glue. It was easy to imagine myself in the place of the respectable bartender, for instance, doling out compassionately liberal measures of tequila, or even in that of the snoring cur under the bar, stealing a few hours of drunken solace from an otherwise unforgiving world. I was warming up to the role of sullen *peón*, brooding over fanciful plots of revenge and violence against a heartless *Don*, when my pint arrived, drawing me back from the bottomless well into which my reflections had carried me.

I paid Billy for the beer, the only person to do so the entire evening, as far as I could tell. Then I took the glass of tarry stout over to one of the empty booths and sat, my back propped against the wall. I had five more pints that night, during which time I talked to no one, and no one talked to me. I was left to wonder what frequency of the social spectrum I inhabited that rendered me so thoroughly invisible to these people.

All I can say is that it would have been better had I not been left to myself and my reflections. Despite the fact that no one was paying me the least regard, I began to feel vaguely threatened, challenged, almost. Not so much by the people—they seemed harmless enough—but by the countless things that their apathy alone (so I thought) allowed to flood existence. It was as if all the inane, discarded things were taunting me with the fact that they had attained the status of being, to the detriment of so many other, more favorable, possibilities. I wracked my brain in an effort to devise some semiotic system according to which I could grant them significance, but came up with nothing.

Obviously, I don't recall all of the thoughts that ran through my mind that night. I do seem to remember staring purposefully at the Mexican mini bar for a long time, maybe fifteen minutes, as if I could compel it to reveal, through force of will alone, the secret of its theurgical power. In any event, by the time I wobbled out the door, I was possessed by feelings of sedition and belligerence. I had resolved to take action, though I wasn't quite sure what. Any doubts I might've had concerning this resolution were wiped away as I stepped outside. For as I crossed the threshold, I swore I heard someone mutter sarcastically, above the general din, "Seeyalatah, Professah," accompanied by a few assenting snickers.

I had just cleared the small, economically depressed business district where *The Shield* was situated and was stomping my way through the residential marches, when I happened upon an object so perfectly suited to bear the brunt of my aimless animus, that for an instant I thought it sent by Divine Providence.

There before me, awash in the lunar glow of it's very own blue and white floodlights, was a two-and-a-half-foot tall, Hohenzollernesque Christ child, complete with ermine cape and Parkay margarine crown. He stood, right hand raised in benediction, upon a river-stone dais, flanked on either side by unpainted cement cherubs. Positioned directly in front of Him, and serving as a sort of storybook bodyguard, was a plywood pumpkin version of Frosty the Snowman.

I was over the short chain link fence in an instant.

I crept stealthily across the yard. Standing before the eerily androgynous statue, I pushed gently against its crowned head, testing its fastness. The statue tilted slightly on its base; it was unsecured. Impulsively, I plucked it from the pedestal and was scrambling back over the fence, taking out the secret service pumpkin man with a well-placed kick to the chest along the way. I ran the rest of the way home with the statue wedged under the crook of my right arm, my face split by a wide, silly grin, my pulse racing to the juvenile prankster's quickened heartbeat.

By the time I had gained the safety of my apartment—the mild psychosis from a year's worth of aesthetic deprivation and idle chatter with the likes of Marie Healy perhaps serving as an impetus—the basic outlines of my master plan had already begun to take shape.

If there's one thing my fellow townspeople seem to care about, one thing they manage to pull off with something like passion or artistry, it's the staging of Catholic statuary. Therefore—or so ran the muddled logic of my questionable syllogism—there could be no better target at which to strike.

Nor, I knew, would there be any shortage of targets. In this town there is some variation on the Virgin-on-the-half-shell motif in practically every fourth yard. A random survey of my neighborhood alone would disclose a veritable who's who of the Catholic Church's most popular saints: Anthony, Jerome, Monica, Jude, Francis, Patrick, Joseph, Padre Pio. The Virginal One Herself, of course, is beyond mere popularity. Our survey would find Mary incarnate (*in concrete*, as it were) as Queen of Heaven, Mother of Sorrows, Immaculate Heart, and as a legion of Our Ladies: of Providence, of Garden Zucchini, of The Street.

The material employed in the construction of suitable saintly residences depends largely on the trade of the house's original owner (the current generation, whether through genuine preference or lack of craft, tend to opt for ready-mades). Thus carpenters built elaborate wooden display cases, complete with Plexiglas windows or doors, masons built impressive stone grottoes and pedestals, bricklayers sunk grottoes into their home's very foundation work.

I had previously taken these monuments, to the extent that I considered them at all, for expressions of an obligatory, populist faith. But that night, I came to see something more sinister behind their seemingly innocent proliferation, namely, idolatry.

It wasn't simply a question of breaking whichever commandment is the "Thou-Shalt-Have-No-Other-Gods-Before-Me" one, though many of my neighbors were undoubtedly guilty of this, judging by the number of mixed-metaphor yards, where saints cohabited with icons of pagan and late capitalist ritual. I'm not exactly what you'd call a Christian, so for me it wasn't a question of the graven images of saints or pagan deities usurping His Glory. No, it seemed to me that I was dealing with a deeper, more fundamental form of idol worship, one in which the very predicament of modern man—or at least that of my neighbors—was implicated.

I conducted a kind of one-man inquest in the ear-ringing silence of my parlor that night, the brightly painted effigy standing for the accused. I sat across the room from the God-Become-Man-Become-Sexless-Statue for hours, sometimes brooding on the enigmatic nature of idolatry, sometimes slipping off into brief bouts of troubled sleep.

It was in the pre-dawn hours of early morning, the pleasant elixir of alcohol and adrenaline long since replaced by a dull, throbbing headache, that the truth came to me, fully formed. Were I a religious person—indeed, were I even so much as an atheist—I might have been inclined to regard the manner of its coming as *mystical*. At the time, however, I found it more reasonable to think of it as the natural product of staunch rationality and disciplined cogitation than as some sort of ecstatic vision. I didn't consider the possibility that it was just my mind regurgitating something I had read long ago.

In any event, *this* was my revelation: In the beginning, the natural world for the most part escaped the indigenous powers of human comprehension. Life, fertility, the cycles of night and day and the seasons, the persistence of stone, calamity, death; all pointed to an extraordinary realm, an unsettling beyond. Not to another place, just to the beyond of comprehension. Call this the human condition. Profane things—rocks, hills, feathers, deformities—came to symbolize this condition, making it manifest and reducing its uncanniness. Idols and images further concentrated this symbolism, becoming sacred things that served as a source of meaning, a refuge from nothingness. This ability to create and maintain a link with transcendence was a truly wondrous power. Enter religion. As a formal collection of sacred objects, a catalogue of their established meanings, religion is nothing but the element of stagnation, the agency by which those objects cease to communicate with the sacred plane and come to be worshipped in themselves. We become their subjects, slaves of our own creations. The ineffable, unutterable God of Christianity, far from representing an evolutionary step forward in the liberation of humanity, is in fact the most completely realized form of this stagnation and enslavement.

Or something to that effect.

I have to confess that I have a difficult time coherently reproducing the whole argument. I do remember that it was perfectly clear to me at the time. Whatever its precise formulation may have been, what was beyond doubt was the conviction that along with this insight came a mandate. I had a role to play, and an important one at that.

I focused on my neighbors. There was no denying that they were mired in the latter stages of this ancient dialectic. That they had fallen from the authentic worship of their God *through* their lawn ornaments to the profane veneration of the statues themselves was clear enough. One had only to recall the yards where virtuous saints, Sacred Hearts ablaze in their cutout chests, shared the stage with Easter Bunnies and Frankenstein Monsters.

What the people of the neighborhood needed, I decided, was to have their direct link with the sacred plane reestablished. What was required for this, I knew, was the systematic debasement of their idols. Which in turn called for a debaser.

I would be that debaser, a latter-day iconoclast, a godless John the Baptist, *vox clamans in deserto*, carrying to them the message they did not want to hear, but would some day thank me for.

I sat there for a little while longer, completely numb. I had come to the most momentous decision of my life. Of course, I had reached this decision hung over, sleep deprived and without the benefit of contrary opinions. So I guess it's understandable that, at the time, I didn't pause to consider the prophet's worldly fate.

I slept through most of the next day, waking late in the afternoon. Filled with purpose, I promptly set about my work. I went first to a garden supply place that sold whimsical garden accoutrements: jolly, corpulent Buddhas; cuddly farm animals; plastic daisy pinwheels; fountains with naked imps peeing endlessly into scalloped-shaped basins. I bought a half-dozen of the items that made me laugh the hardest. Next, I went to the local ACE hardware and picked up some tools that seemed likely to come in handy. Then I headed home to further prepare myself and wait for midnight.

The first night went exactly as I had envisioned it, almost as if the unseen hand of a favorably disposed spirit was guiding my actions. After a ceremonial meal of vegetable broth, Triscuits and cream soda, I waited for the violet glow from Marie's second floor window to be extinguished, signifying the conclusion of Leno and her retirement for the evening. It would not do to be surveilled by the neighborhood snoop before my work had even begun. I tossed the new tools into my knapsack, selected one of the garden objects, and headed off into the night.

I strolled casually through the deserted, orange-tinted streets, seemingly without purpose. As a matter of fact, I had no particular target in mind; I would know it, I knew, when I came to it.

Around the corner and two blocks down from my place, I came to it. It was mounted atop a large cement base into which were set rough, jagged rocks. I had no idea who or what the statue depicted, as its owners had mummified it against the harsh winter weather with countless layers of cellophane. I calmly let myself through the front gate and walked serenely across the yard to the shimmering polymer obelisk.

Unlike the statue the night before, this one didn't budge. It had been bolted to a wooden plank, which was in turn set into the cement. I was prepared for this eventuality. I took a socket wrench from my shoulder bag and quickly removed the four 5/8" bolts, finding myself remarkably untroubled by the loud ratcheting sound. I took the statue from its stand with a crinkling of plastic, setting it on the ground while I respectfully reinserted the bolts. Then I gathered my tools and headed home with the statue under my arm, having left in its place a truly devilish Bunny Boy, with intense, haunting eyes.

When I got home I put the statue, still shrink-wrapped, in the parlor next to the Christ-It. I had another bowl of broth and then went to bed. For the first time since I can remember, I slept peacefully, without dreams.

I followed the same routine for the next five nights, adding a St. Monica, a St. Peter, two identical St. Anthonys, and of all things, a St. Bernard of Clairvaux to my gallery. In their stead were placed a truly thought-provoking group of figures. Each time my work went off without a hitch.

Until tonight.

Tonight I returned to *The Shield*. As before, I went with an ulterior motive: I was anxious for word of my activities, to find out if my work was having any kind of impact. Perhaps, I reasoned, a little eavesdropping in the bar would prove fruitful in this regard.

Compared to my first visit, the bar was nearly empty. There were only about eight people inside, including the dour Billy Martin. The booth where I sat before was occupied by an amorous, chain smoking barfly couple I had often seen passed out in the local park, so I grabbed a stool near the far end of the bar and waited for Billy to drag himself over.

To my right sat a skinny, Irish-style kid—honestly, he looked to be about eighteen—smoking menthol cigarettes and drinking shots of Sambuca. He was wearing an expensive-looking, powder blue tracksuit, the pants of which were tucked into unscathed, loosely tied work boots. His reddish hair was close-cropped on top and completely shaved from the temples down on the sides. He had supplemented his boyish high school moustache with a sparse, wiry chin beard. The fair, sensitive skin of his face was red and blotchy from countless patches of painful looking acne. His body language communicated nothing but tension and a violence that was never far from the surface. Indeed, he was bouncing his leg on the stool's footrest with such speed and intensity that little shock waves traveled all the way up the bar and spread across the foamy surface of my Guinness.

To my left sat the same handful of people as before, under the attentive supervision of the venerable Trinitron. The classic made-for-TV movie *Killdozer* had just started. For some reason, the set's volume had been turned off and the closed-caption mode activated. Accordingly, the people next me paid no attention to the movie and instead just stared into their drinks.

I, for one, found the movie quite enjoyable. Especially as every few minutes the ever-dwindling construction crew somehow managed to stumble across the path of the possessed bulldozer. Each time this happened, the lights of the demonic machine would flash on and off ominously, and the white lettering at the bottom of the screen would read: [HORN HONKING]. Then Killdozer's exhaust pipe would belch menacingly: [RUMBLE,RUMBLE]. The gears would shift under the guidance of an invisible hand: [VROOOM!VROOOM!]. Finally, one of the hard-hatted workers would come to his senses and yell: ["LET'S GET OUTTA HERE!!!"].

It was clear that I was in the wrong place to hear news of my work. I still seemed to be flying under the locals' social radar, and I once again spent the evening in complete silence. Admittedly, it had been a stupid idea to begin with.

But I stayed on anyway, if only to watch the rest of the movie. I drained pint after pint, and by the time it had ended and I got up to leave, I was actually quite drunk. A week of broth and crackers had not exactly fortified me against the effects of alcohol. A brisk walk home in the cold night air, I thought, would do me good.

I was about halfway home when I came across the Mother of all Mother of God statues. It was housed in a humble, store-bought grotto, far below the standards of grandeur to which I had become accustomed. But there was something about her, something alluring, provocative. It could have been the perfectly painted flesh colored skin, or her strangely sultry face, made-up with red lipstick, blue eye shadow and rouged cheeks. My tools and ritualistic serenity conspicuously absent, I plowed through the leafless shrubs at the edge of the yard and stumbled over to the statue.

To my delight I found that she actually had glass eyes, like a doll's, brown and mysterious. Here, I thought, was the epitome of all that my work was aimed against. I kissed it right on its frozen red lips.

I grabbed it then and turned to leave, but before I knew it, I had fallen and was lying face first in the dead grass. *Am I that drunk?* I thought. As I started to get up, I felt a slight tug on my left ankle. I looked down to see it loosely tangled in a length of high-test fishing line.

I had just finished extricating my foot when I noticed that I was squinting: the yard was flooded with intense white light. I froze like the proverbial deer. Only gradually did I become aware of the sound of an alarm, a robotic female voice calling out repeatedly, "Burg-a-ler! Burg-a-ler! Burg-a-ler!"

I was struggling for comprehension when, almost in unison, first-floor lights in all of the neighboring houses went on and I understood: they had organized.

I got up quickly, grabbed the Madonna and took off down the street, back in the direction of The Shield. I could hear the ancient, rusty springs of screen doors being flung open behind me. But I had gotten a decent jump on them and knew I was home free.

I had just passed *The Shield*, my initially solid form already deteriorating into the aforementioned waddle, when I realized I was running the wrong way. I stopped suddenly, as if in a trance. Instead of looking for a suitable detour, however, I walked back toward the bar, overtaken by a powerful urge. I entered, flinging the door open wildly, and strode to the middle of the room, the statue raised above my head. All was silence and closed-captioning and gently wafting cigarette smoke. Everyone was staring at me intently. Then I yelled out: "THE TIME HAS COME!!! WAKE UP TO YOURSELVES!!!"

Drunken silence. A tubercular cough.

The blotchy kid tittered, stubbing out his cigarette in the ashtray next to him. Then he said, in a falsetto voice that was nonetheless quite chilling, "Aw-ight, buddy. That's nice. How 'bout you wake up to me beatin' ya head wif ya girlfren'?"

I came back to myself.

I turned and ran, thinking, *I can still get out of this.*

Their minds and bodies unaccustomed to action, the patrons of *The Shield* shuffled out onto the sidewalk about ten seconds behind me, just in time to join forces with the neighborhood watch.

~

So here I am. Cowering beneath the leafless sanctuary of a weeping cherry, my swollen left knee getting stiffer by the minute. The mob is just a few houses down, retrieving the headless statue from the yard into which I had tossed it. One of the guys heaves it to and hands it to another, patting him on the back reassuringly. Then they all turn and begin walking slowly in my direction, coming to a halt just a few yards from me. I limp out from under the tree as best I can, trying to make it seem like I was hiding more out of cunning than cowardice.

I feel the weight of numerous denials pressing down on me: I can't believe they caught me. I can't believe I was so deluded to think anything would come of my ridiculous "mission." I can't believe I chose such a lame place to hide. I can't believe I'm here.

It looks like everyone who was in *The Shield*, with the exception of the alcoholic couple, has survived the chase: the Trinitron crew, the blotchy kid, even Billy Martin. *Who's watching the bar?* I can already feel the seeds of a deep depression germinating over the shame of being apprehended by this lot.

Not that there's any honor in being caught by the neighborhood watch. There are six of them, and they don't exactly look like triathletes. They're all in their late forties, short, a little on the portly side, and still out of breath from the chase. And they're all equally grimy. It's like a brotherhood of tow truck drivers. Not that they don't look angry enough to be dangerous. After all, I've defiled their religion *and* their property. Worse yet, I've kept them up late and forced them to lumber after me for about a mile.

They're standing around me expectantly, apparently waiting for me to say something. Six drunks, six tow truck drivers. A jury of my peers. This, then, is the group in whose hands my fate rests. I suppose I've no right to expect better, but I can't help drawing unfortunate parallels to the troop of gibbering morons that Bosch chose to escort a somnolent Christ to His Destiny.

I'm thinking maybe it's not too late to change my approach a little. Be apologetic, maybe. Or just try to laugh it off as a harmless prank, invent a friend that I could say put me up to it.

I nod at the guy holding the remains. "You set all that up yourself?" I ask. "The alarms and the lights?" I'm hoping at least to communicate my grudging respect.

"Yeah, I did. Well, we all did," he says, indicating the crowd behind him.

"Betcha didn't see that comin', did ya smaht ass?" Blotchy's the only one in this crowd who really worries me.

"You must be the one who took my St. Jerome, too. Was it you?"

"I don't know. Maybe. Is he all wrapped in plastic?"

"Yeah."

"Then yes, I'm pretty sure I have your Jerome. He . . . it . . . it's unharmed, if you want to know. Still wrapped up, actually. They're all OK. Look, I'm willing to give them all back. They're all completely undamaged." I look down at the head in my hands. "Except for this one, I guess. Sorry. I'll buy you a new one"

There's no response. Only a quiet, uncertain indifference. Maybe my sincere and apologetic tone *has* disarmed them. Maybe I really can get out of this by playing it straight. But beneath that hope I can feel myself getting angry. This is exactly the kind of apathy I set out to undo. I decide, at the eleventh hour, to remain faithful to my mission, to stick it out to the bitter end. I hold the head up for them to see.

"But, I mean, just look at this. What the hell are you people doing? She has *eyelashes*. Lipstick. Rouge. This is supposed to be a *representation* of the mother of your God. The symbol of a miraculous power. Not a show girl."

"But what's more beautiful than the mother of Jesus?"

"*Exactly*. But, you see, the motherhood part's symbolic. The beauty too. It's not supposed to be porn star beauty."

"You're sick, dude."

"I'm just saying that it's *all* symbolic. It's supposed to be an embodiment of all of the mysteries of your religion. And all those religious stories are just metaphorical versions of what are ultimately *human* mysteries. They don't come from some white-haired super being in the clouds."

"You think we don't know that?"

I'm a little thrown by that one. I'm also having trouble distinguishing between the neighborhood watch guys. They're pretty much interchangeable, as far as I can tell.

"Well, I don't know. I guess maybe I don't think you do."

One of the tow truck guys—I'm pretty sure he hasn't spoken yet—actually raises his hand.

Incredulous, I motion for him to go ahead.

"So, you took my motha-in-lawr's St. Moniker?" Some of them, apparently, are bit slower than others.

"Yes."

"And put a ET in its place?"

"Yes."

"Is that s'posed to be some kinda joke?" He has the same blinking eye thing as Marie.

"No, not really."

"What're you tryin' ta do? Why'd you take my motha-in-lawr's statue? You know, she's elda-ly, and infirm. She prays to her Moniker every day. It's the only thing that gives her hope and solace."

"It's a fuckin' hate crime dude, s'what it is." Blotchy has made his way to the front of the group.

"Why'd you do it?"

Blinky really wants to know. Should I tell them the truth? I suppose now is as good a time as any to deliver my message.

"Look. You know what an iconoclast is, right?"

Knitted brows. A shifty, grade school silence.

I'm thinking of rephrasing the question when Billy Martin, of all people, pipes up: "It's a Dodge van, right?" He looks at the others for support. "You know, the big one?"

Blotchy shakes his head impatiently. "Naw, you fuckin' dildo, it's a dude that smashes religious shit, like this fag."

He's really starting to get under my skin. "Hey look, just shut up, will you? I'm trying to explain something important here."

He shrugs his shoulders.

I can sense that *this* is my moment, my brief window of opportunity. These next few moments will define my time on this planet. I wish I felt a bit more charismatic. But it's not hopeless; these people—some of them, anyway—are more intelligent than I initially gave them credit for. Maybe my message *will* make sense to them. Maybe it will even come as a kind of recognition, a confirmation of something they have themselves suspected all along.

"What do you really know about the idols you place in your yards?"

"They're Saints, not idols. We're not pygmies."

"Let me put it this way. Are you happy with the world, the way it is, with your place in it?"

They turn to each other, chuckling.

The guy holding the statue looks at me with tired eyes and says, "The world is what it is, we ah what we ah. It's not about happiness."

"But that's where you're wrong. At the most fundamental level, all of us, all human beings, are creators. The world around us is *our* creation, not God's. Sure, we didn't fashion it, it had to come from somewhere, and we'll probably never truly understand how it came about, but why should we care? *That's* why your statues are idols. Because you think they point to real gods and concrete miracles, that they are these gods and miracles. But that's not how they started out. They started out as things that let us accept what was beyond our grasp and focused our creative power on the creation of *our* world. This is the ultimate truth, that . . ."

I'm interrupted by a shrill, MIDI version of *Ride Of The Valkyries*. It's Blotchy's mobile phone. He pulls a small silver device from the front pouch of his tracksuit and lets it ring a couple more times before answering it: "Yeah? S'up? Yeah? Yeah. Uh-hunh. Uh-hunh. Nunh-unh. No, man. No, man, fuck that. Fuck that shit. Hunh? Yeah, aw-ight. Aw-ight. No, man, fuck huh. No . . . no . . . look, man, I'm busy. Just busy, man . . . I'm in the middle a sumpthin'. I don't know, man, few minutes maybe. I don't know, yeah. No man, fuck huh . . . look, jus' tell huh, tell that little bitch to wait five minutes, aw-ight? No, man, alls I'm sayin' is wait five minutes, aw-ight? Aw-ight. Yeah, aw-ight. Yeah, layta."

Slowly, silently, everyone returns their attention to me. I sense that they actually *want* me to continue.

I clear my throat, trying to remember where I had left off. I can feel my already slight hold on things slipping away.

"Don't you see? I was just trying to give you a chance to reclaim something sacred. The purpose of sacred objects, like what your statues *could* be, is to protect people, to protect you, from the strange, from the unknown. But in the end, what you're doing with all this is directing repression against yourself, against your own ability to be . . ."

"You ah evuhl."

Things are not going to end up in my favor.

I give it one last shot: "Sure, I'll admit it. I'm evil. But that's what I'm trying to say. Being evil's part of being human. Maybe even the best part. It's only when we deny this fundamental part of ourselves that we get into . . ."

His eyes rolling in disbelief, Blotchy's apparently heard enough. "C'mon! Will you listen to this shit?!" He throws his hands up in exasperation, then assumes a mocking tone: "*In the end*, the purpose of not bein' a *faggot* is to protect you from gettin' your ass kicked when you come from outta town and steal people's shit."

I have no response to this line of argumentation. I look about the assembly. They're getting cold, bored, sober. I suspect the ambiguity of the situation is intolerable to them. I've made the wrong play. If I had just stuck with the apologetic tone, they might have been willing to take their property back and forget about it. Nothing I've said, nothing I've done, has made the least bit of an impact.

What was I thinking?

The worst part is, I've lost a theological disputation with Blotchy. Now—his sense of timing really is impeccable—he delivers the *coup de grâce*: "Let's just pound this fuckin' gaybo and go back to the fuckin' bah!"

I feel martyrdom approaching.

For some reason, an image of Messina's *Martyrdom of St. Sebastian* comes to mind. Maybe it has to do with the fact that Sebastian is, among other things, the patron saint of neighborhood watch programs. Or perhaps it's an unconscious recommendation of the stance I should assume in the face of my doom. Not a bad role model. Clad only in a pair of strangely modern-looking panties, Sebastian's pose is one of utter relaxation and indifference. He stands languidly before the trunk of a tree, to which he is bound apparently only as a matter of decorum. His body betrays not so much as a tensed muscle, despite the bolts piercing his thigh and torso. I think maybe he derives this strength and courage not so much from his knowledge of the world to come and his place in it, as from the ultimate honor of being the center of a Renaissance composition.

But this is not the Renaissance. It's not even the Middle Ages. My imminent martyrdom will not be a highbrow, aesthetic experience. It will provide the subject of no artistic studies. It will be an anonymous, survivable, and, most likely, well-deserved beating. A bloody nose, a chipped tooth, a swollen lip, some torn clothing.

The group, which to a man has assumed an unambiguously aggressive posture, begins closing in on me.

I'm struck by a feeling of *déjà vu* so strong my ears start ringing. I feel a supernatural chill settle in my bones. The realization dawns slowly: this is a scene is straight out of one of my recurrent childhood nightmares. In this frightening dream, it's night. I awaken in a dark, empty house, an utterly uncanny house that is nevertheless recognizable as my own. Sensing it to be unsafe, I rush into the street and begin wandering through my neighborhood, completely naked. I go from house to house looking for help, only to discover that everyone in my neighborhood, my parents included, is actually a fundamentalist, disciplinarian zombie. I flee in terror, doing my best to escape them, but they're relentless and there are just too many of them. Inevitably, I find myself cornered by dozens of crazed, leering, zombie neighbors. My complete terror at the prospect of being torn limb from limb and devoured is offset by impotent shame at my public nakedness. It was at this point in the nightmare that I always woke up, or transitioned into another, less malignant, dream.

I'm half expecting such an improbable segue now, though I know none is coming. There'll be no waking up from this one. The circle tightens slowly. *Why are they being so cautious?* I wish I were home reading. I have the hollow feeling of having lived my life, unwittingly, for no other purpose than to fulfill the nightmares of a boy I no longer remember. And if I interpret the zombie nightmare correctly, it seems I never felt at home, even as a kid. Maybe the problem is not with the world but with me. Maybe I really don't belong here. That here. This here. Any here. I open my hands—the head falling to the ground like a former life—and let them come.

virus worms

I offer an answer: "esophagus?"
"Yeah, asophagus. Right. You're right."
Now, he knows that the tube running from the mouth to the stomach is called the esophagus. But he's figured it out: pretending that he doesn't know offers the best chance of keeping the game going. So long as the words are spoken aloud, the game stays out in the open. It keeps the hooks in us, too, this little pretense of his. Forced to respond to these *rhetorical* questions, we're still part of the game.

Not that we mind playing. Not at all. The car is enveloped by his imagination, it's like breathing an alien atmosphere. It sustains and hobbles us. And it's infectious. Already, the trees along the highway are looking more like neurons and bronchioles to me than trees, the tail lights of the cars ahead of us more like red blood cells than halogen bulbs sheathed in red plastic, proximity beacons aimed at the half-seeing eyes of weary travelers.

Then our son is on his knees in the back seat, pointing to the road up ahead. "There's another one! There's a virus!"

We got a late start from the city, leaving a house full of friends only half an hour earlier. It's now almost 8:00 on a Sunday night, tomorrow a school day. The kid is tired. We're tired. Privately, we entertain the fantasy of him acknowledging his weariness, wishing us a fond good night and curling up in his blanket to sleep out the long journey home.

But it's not to be.

We're hardly outside the city limits when the game begins. We are not in a car stuck in traffic. We're leukocytes, intrepid white blood cells patrolling the highways and byways of the human body. We're on the prowl for foreign invaders, viruses mostly, cruising our host's bloodstream. They're easy to spot: a broken tail light, a flashing turn signal, a hulking Suburban. We get these intruders in the sights of our thumb-and-forefinger bio-laser guns and then blast them, unraveling their RNA.

He's a savvy little guy. He knows that a simple adventure game such as this is enough to pull us in. Sure, his imagination creates a bridge to the private thoughts of our own childhood. But he also knows he's walking a fine line.

Adventure requires violence, and he knows we're not about to condone a gratuitous, full-bore shoot out, even if it is on a cellular level.

He therefore adds a pedagogical twist to the game. The highway is intersected every few miles by quaint overpasses, New Deal era jobs of concrete and stone. Each overpass is unique. Our son pulls this topographical feature into the game: each time we drive beneath an overpass actually signifies our passage into a different part of the body. This gives the game an educational slant. How could any parent reasonably resist an anatomical adventure game?

So we're playing the game, driving along and zapping viruses and moving from one part of the body to the next. For the most part, the sequence of body parts triggered by the traversal of overpasses is anatomically correct. We go through the nasal cavity down to the throat, from there we plunge down the esophagus into the... *brain?*

The game goes off the rails for a moment. We exchange mildly concerned glances. We know that he knows the body. He's always loved the body, especially the systems of organs and, above all, the skeleton. Surely he hasn't forgotten that the esophagus doesn't lead to the brain? Besides, we're enjoying the game, we're comfortable with the rules that have been established. We're even reconciled to the fact of his being awake and alarmingly alert. The last thing we want now is the arbitrary devolution into absurdity that tired six-year olds have been known to introduce into their play.

But then he points out that the bridge under which we had just passed *looked* like a brain. I look over my shoulder at the receding overpass and it *does* look like a brain, its surface carved in a strange, wavy relief. This seems an acceptable deviation, to move about the body based on the resemblances of certain overpasses to various body parts, rather than via anatomical sequence. We nod to each other, relieved, and continue with the game.

It's now 8:40. The game goes on, unabated. The most recent twist is that we are now a crew of white blood cells, patrolling the body in a microscopic submarine. Accordingly, we now have titles. My wife, who happens to be driving the submarine, is of course the navigator. By some stroke of luck, I have been designated captain of our sturdy vessel. Our son demurely accepts the role of lieutenant. He's not reading yet, but has nevertheless managed to acquire a knowledge of military hierarchy.

More importantly, the game is now essentially a monologue being conducted from the back seat. It's far too dark to make out most of the game's erstwhile external features: trees, buildings, overpasses. All that's left are the lights of other cars. In other words, our son's imagination need not make any concessions to the outside world. Apparently, only constant chatter allows him to keep up with the pace of his invention. We are occasionally consulted on matters of vocabulary, technology, probability. But at this point, it's the questions that count, not the answers, and any responses we do offer tend to be drowned out in a torrent of neo-babble.

We begin thinking of ways to bring the game to a close. We begin scanning the exits for fast food restaurants.

A weekend spent at the home of friends in the city. Friends unaware of the peculiar proclivities and aversions of the six-year old palate. Friends whose pantry is therefore not stocked with ketchup and pickle relish, with hard boiled eggs (yolks only) and skinned hot dogs, with crackers and crab dip, kalamata olives and ginger ale.

8:50 on a Sunday night seems a fine time to eat. Chicken nuggets, fries and maybe a milk seems a fine meal this once. In and out, quick. He eats, the game loses momentum, we seize the opportunity to cajole him off to sleep.

We're a moderately democratic body, so the idea of taking a break from our mission in order to obtain some nourishment is put forth to the crew. "OK captain," says the lieutenant. "Sounds like a good idea."

A fast food franchise is easily located. We pull off the highway and I dive into the restaurant. It's intensely lit, and empty, apart from the Salvadoran crew standing forlornly behind the counter. A long way from home. I order the kid's-meal version of chicken and fries, substituting the soft drink with milk.

"No milk."

"Can I buy it on the side, then?"

She looks over her shoulder, as if to indicate the restaurant in its entirety, and says again, "No milk."

I get fruit punch and return to the car.

9:04. We're back on the road. Our son's meal has been arranged as economically as possible: chicken nuggets and fries in one half of the box, ketchup in the other, fruit punch in a nearby cup cozy. Over the humming of the engine, the sweet sound of small lips smacking together can be heard.

And then: "Good chow, captain!"

Even now, the game cannot be allowed to end. The car interior is aglow with the red lights of the microscopic sub's control panel. Outside, *in the body*, all is black. The imagination wins.

For some reason, the whole thing reminds me of the Taoist parable of the man who, upon waking from a dream that he was a butterfly, was no longer sure whether he was a man dreaming he was a butterfly or a butterfly dreaming he was a man. The difference is that our son, unlike the man, doesn't care to know which.

Still trying to guide the game to a conclusion, we inquire as to the quality of the fries.

"No, no. They're not french fries. They're wire-us worms."

"They're *what?*"

"You know, wire-us worms."

The window of time here, to avoid stigmatizing the boy, not to mention my appearing less than omniscient to him, is brief. It is about to close and then, recognition.

"Ohhhh. You mean *virus* worms?"

"Yeah, wire-us worms."

"Oh, okay. Well, how are the virus worms?"

"Good! Tastes just like french fries!"

old

For as long as I can remember, I wanted to be old. Not just older, bigger, like my siblings and cousins; it wasn't a question of my being the youngest. I wanted to *be old*, like the grandparents, great uncles and aunts and other, even more distant, relatives that haunted our holidays and family gatherings.

From the start, these living ghosts exerted a strange force of attraction upon me, one to which I can never recall offering the slightest resistance. Taking advantage of a certain indeterminacy of age—I was at once too old to coddle and too young to warrant the gruff admonitions that would've been leveled at the older kids—I willfully violated the adult space of the parlor, wandering eccentric orbits about the grown-up's knees as they stood in small groups, engaged in frivolous gossip or grim and worrisome political debate.

Not once did the battery of formulaic expressions of fondness and disdain that attended my initial appearance—the hair-tusslings and cheek-pinchings; the scratchy kisses from ancient mouths, painted red and bordered by prickly silver hairs; the resentful glares from work-hardened faces, the kind that find a measure of satisfaction only in the pain or misfortune of others—not once did this seem too high a price to pay for the privilege of observing these archaic and alien beings up close.

I drifted through the parlor's strange haze—a thanosphere of cigarette smoke and drugstore perfume, of camphor and unwashed skin, of breath heavy with bitters and fortified wine—all the while clandestinely attentive to the old ones' movements and gestures. Stiff, slow, aimless, as if their sole purpose was the consumption of time.

Eventually, I would make my way to the parlor's remote corners and dark recesses, where the day's host would have stationed second-hand easy chairs, hauled from storage and hastily tidied for the occasion in question. The forest of legs grew thin as I drew near these musty outposts, the hum of conversation vague and distant. And there they sat, the oldest of the old, forgotten, having long since succumbed to sleep, their impossible faces waxen, arid mouths agape.

Having not, as yet, been properly instructed in the fear of death, I had no sense of the realm, intermediate between the sacred and the profane, which I had entered. I knew nothing of shame or transgression. I had simply followed my heart, or something like instinct, to the place where I most wanted to be; a researcher in the field, a fetishist in the secret vault housing his collection.

I approached the slumbering relics cautiously, not out of fear, but from a sacramental deference born of utter fascination. There was nothing about them that failed to compel me, not even the scratchy clothing that hung loosely, like the flesh it covered, from the bones of their spare frames, typically in strange combinations of pure happenstance. I poked their limbs through the rough, sober fabric of their clothing, marveling at the nearness of their skeletons. I even admired their irritability, on those occasions when my prodding recalled them from the weightless near-death of sleep to the dreadful gravity of their bodies, delighted in the swift surfacing of their bitterness, welcomed the punishments—a slap, a cuff, an old-world curse—that were more the products of reflex than any exercise of will. Otherwise I stared at their faces, the terrible, quivering totems of my private religion; faces as incomprehensible to me, at first, as the cuneiform tablets must have been to those who pulled them from the formless mounds of the Sumerian desert.

I explored these glyphs with infinite patience. The milky, watery eyes, the skin hanging from bony prominences like surplus parchment, the structural collapse of cheeks, chins, earlobes. I became a cartographer of this cruel terrain, seeing not faces but maps in topographical relief: the lines etched deeply into the skin like valleys; the dark, swollen barrows beneath the eyes; the random hillocks of pre-cancerous growths; the fine network of blood vessels, rivers and streams that, contrary to those found in nature, work their way *toward* the surface with the passage of time.

Lacking a legend or supplemental inscription to aid interpretation, it was inevitable that I should come to regard these features as artifacts, the residual consequence of the subjection of the human form to something like geologic time. To a slow, steady, imperceptible violence.

I devised the theory that the trappings of old age were in fact the symbols of an elaborate cipher, one in which some terrible, fantastic secret was encoded. A secret which the old themselves were neither inclined nor compelled to share with anyone else. They were an exiled race, it seemed to me, without stake in human affairs; out of step with time, and thus somehow outside meaning and the order of things.

Standing there before them, I would effect what I perceived to be the essence of their manner—the apparent fatigue, the forsaken mien, the labored breathing that seemed like a language in itself—as if, through emulation alone, I hoped to unlock the secret I had so recently attributed to them.

It was only later—so much later—that I came to realize that it was in fact the hands of my ancient relations—long since dead, of course—that had fascinated me all along.

Hands the first task of which had been to reconcile the unbound ego with the irrefutable but always uncanny fact of its extension in space. Hands that circumscribed the margins—and limitations—of that ego's physical being, signaling the advent of time, the imposition of finitude. Hands that would later become the instruments of a petty revenge upon the matter with which the ego competes for space, tooling the natural world, hammering and bending and shaping metal and wood and stone into forms that serve. Hands that endlessly worked lathe, press and saw. Hands that could not, for all that, stop the march of time, the constant application of force upon the matter of our bodies.

Thus hands bent and gnarled, spotted and scarred, hands stripped of fingers and sapped of strength. Hands shaped by time into books that we could read, if we cared to. The true maps of our personal histories, our solitary wanderings, our struggles.

It was the hands of the old, then, that I sought to understand, that I had hoped, unwittingly, to emulate. The hands of the old, I would come to realize, held the key to the secret that had so puzzled me. I realized this only because I too had grown old. Because, imperceptibly, their hands had become my hands.

swing

THE PADDED 5X7 ENVELOPE HAD NO RETURN ADDRESS. Not that it needed one. Grace knew that I would recognize the handwriting, knew that her knowing I knew she would know was already half the message. I suppose I might have taken some solace in the realization that she was still alive—up to the date on the post-mark, anyway. To be honest, however, I never remotely entertained the possibility of foul play; that's what the police were for. And their musings on the subject ran only so far as to how they could implicate me. I don't hold it against them. In their experience, the man at the other end of a missing woman is always either a sorry cuckold or a sociopath. They would have been inclined, I think, to write me off as the former, had it not been for Gordon's efforts to convince them otherwise. I don't hold it against him, either. I would have expected nothing less from a man with both feet planted firmly in the real world.

Nor did I feel even a momentary tinge of the smug satisfaction that usually accompanies being right. You see, I had maintained all along—if only because I really had no other choice—that Grace was gone, not missing, that whatever mystery lay behind her disappearance was of a personal, not a criminal, nature. The arrival of the envelope seemed to support my position.

In truth, what little comfort I derived from the package had to do with the fact that, as far as communication was concerned, she hadn't changed. A positive sign, I thought. She was as sparing, as effortlessly parsimonious in her transmission of information as ever. The package—the sum total of whatever was on or in the envelope—would contain information enough for me to understand what she wanted me to. I might not get it immediately—I might not even get it at all—but I wouldn't come to know more than she intended.

I sat in the kitchen for a while, staring at the yellow-green envelope on the table before me, at the blood-red ink of the post-mark, at my name, hovering alone over *our* address, laid down by her hand in dark blue, her immaculate script as regular as a typeface. I sighed loudly, as if trying to prompt someone to inquire after my well being.

It was pointless, of course. I was, once again, completely alone.

I closed my eyes, pressing my thumb and forefinger against the lids to dispel the envelope's ghostly afterimage. At length, I opened them again, blinked a blink of resolve and took up the package.

And yet, I could do no better than interrogate it absently, turning it over in my hands, running my fingers along its surface, holding it up to my nose.

It didn't really matter. A thorough forensic analysis wouldn't have turned up much more than my half-hearted investigation. According to the postmark, it had been mailed four days ago, from a post office in Graeburn, a small town upstate. That was it. No return address, as I said. No other markings of any kind. No distinct aroma, no potentially meaningful choice of postage stamp. The fact that it had been mailed remained, for the time being, the only information of real significance.

I broke the seal painstakingly, like a spendthrift hoping to preserve the envelope for reuse, and applied a gentle pressure to its reinforced edges with the fingertips of my right hand. Its mouth yawned open and I tilted it slightly. A single MiniDisc cartridge slid softly into my left palm. The handwriting on the disc's label, also hers, read:

FOREST LAWN PLAYGROUND | T.F. | 04.19.72

I had no problem making sense of the first line. It most likely corresponded to the series of field recordings she had been making for Gordon at the time of her disappearance. The initials "t.f." called nothing immediately to mind, so I decided not to worry about their possible importance for the time being. The date, however, presented something of a discrepancy. At first glance, it seemed to indicate that whatever was on the disc was thirty years old—almost to the day in fact—while the latest of her recent playground recordings was made but six weeks ago, around the time I last saw her. There was also the obvious fact that MiniDisc wasn't around in 1972, so most likely she had simply transferred a thirty-year old recording from some other medium, one that would have been too cumbersome to mail, or which I might have found impossible, for lack of equipment or know-how, to play. It was also possible that the date bore no relation to the contents of the disc at all. Assuming, of course, that there was even anything on it.

But these possibilities, I knew, had nothing to do with the heart of the matter. They were merely technical considerations, contrived to shield me from the obvious: what I was being confronted with was a message from the past. From her past.

And that was tacitly against the rules. We had always been of one mind as far as the need for a moratorium on the divulging of pasts—or the inquiring into them, for that matter—was concerned. This agreement was based on our shared belief that the past had no real purpose, that it could be little more than a thorn in the side of the present. As with all of our promises, spoken or otherwise, we had never come close to breaking this one.

And then, like the inexorable fulfillment of some family curse, the very message that confirms my belief—that she's gone—arrives from the past.

~

It seemed obvious that the first thing was to play the disc. So, without having given a thought to whether I actually wanted to hear it or not, I found myself heading across the yard to the converted tool shed Grace used for a studio.

It was a cold, early spring day. A steady, pointless drizzle fell from a sullen gray sky. I could feel the dread atmosphere leeching my already weak sense of purpose with each step. *What was the point of this? What would I gain by finding out? Would it change the fact that she was most likely not coming back? Would it make a difference to me?*

I was only about halfway across the yard when it occurred to me that the best course of action would be for me to fall in a heap, right there on the soggy ground, let the rain break me down into my constituent parts, enzymes and proteins and amino acids flowing apart, washed away until all trace of me had disappeared. And memory, too. Especially memory. Whatever molecular aberration is responsible for memory, dissolved and dispersed into little muddy puddles. As it was, I just stood there for a few long moments, motionless, my coat and shoes covered by a shimmering layer of fine rain droplets.

I can be forgiven, I think, for that little breakdown. I wouldn't tend to characterize myself as a particularly strong person, whatever the register, but I think my behavior through this ordeal has been, in a way, admirable. Up to that moment, I had dealt with it all—Grace's unexplained disappearance, Gordon's antics, the police—with the singular resolve, the unflappable rationality, of a madman. Grace would have been impressed.

Basically, my immediate concern, when confronted with her sudden absence, was not for her, but for *us*. It wasn't selfishness, strictly speaking. She would have responded in the same way, I believe, were our positions reversed. I just made a semi-conscious decision to focus my energies, above all else, on keeping our universe intact.

Here's the story, to the extent that it exists. One night six weeks ago, Grace went out. She had no pre-arranged plans, so far as I knew. She didn't say a word about where she was going, or why, and I didn't ask. She didn't need a reason to come and go as she wanted. We were both free to do as we liked, as far as that was concerned. It wasn't uncommon for her to head off, at any hour of the day or night, in pursuit of some recording or other, though in this instance I didn't notice the canvas rucksack filled with equipment that always accompanied her on such impromptu outings. She could just as well have been heading out to the bookstore. Or maybe she was meeting some friends for a drink. Less likely, I thought, but not impossible.

So I had no reason to be particularly worried when I rolled over in bed later that night, forcing my eyes open long enough to see the clock's glowing red 3:40, and she was still not home. The next day came and went, and although I certainly wondered what she might be up to, I still wasn't particularly alarmed.

Two days later, I was concerned. Despite my apprehension, however, I was unable to picture Grace in any sort of trouble, or at least what you might call conventional trouble, the kind that would require my *doing* something. She was a sovereign being. Nothing would happen to her against her will.

I guess even then I had already resolved—though not entirely consciously—to play this one a bit unorthodox, choosing instead what most people would consider a peculiar course: I chose to wait.

Then Gordon called.

Grace had failed to show up for a project status meeting that morning, something that never happened. He asked if I knew where she was, or how he could get hold of her. I told him that I hadn't heard from her for a couple days. He sounded a little confused, then asked me to let her know he called, and hung up.

A couple of minutes later, he called again.

Wasn't I worried about not hearing from her for so long? No, not particularly. *Had I called around?* No, I hadn't. *Had I contacted the police, or the Highway Patrol?* No, I hadn't. *Had we had a fight?* No, we hadn't.

Sensing that he was getting nowhere, he hung up in a huff.

The next afternoon, after a couple more ineffectual phone calls, he showed up at my front door, informing me, in all seriousness, that we *needed to talk*.

I saw no harm in letting him in. I wasted a few minutes brewing the pot of coffee that television has taught uninvited guests to expect, then brought two large cups of it into the living room. Gordon put enough cream and sugar in his to turn it into a child's treat, then blew into it desperately. He sat there across the living room from me, cradling the cup in both hands, looking for all the world like someone who had just survived a wilderness ordeal.

He started talking.

"I understand your reluctance to act, Garret, your fear. I really do." He looked at me with unfathomable earnestness. "But you have to get over that and think about Grace here."

I should have peed in his cup.

"I haven't stopped thinking about Grace, Gordon."

"Of course not, Garret. That's not what I meant. But she needs our help. We need to do something. *You* need to do something, Garret."

"She's a grown-up, Gordon, she doesn't need anyone's help. She'll come back when she wants." I was circumspect with my tone, careful that it betray not one iota of concern.

He pressed on, but by that point, my role in the conversation was already over. I had nothing to say, so I didn't say it. I was barely even listening to his continued talking—something about *mobilizing his network of friends into a grass roots search effort*—wondering instead how much time he spent each morning getting his hair so calculatedly disheveled.

For a number of reasons, Gordon was already inclined to think poorly of me. At first he devoured my reticence happily, taking it for evidence of the weakness he wanted to see in me. Clearly, *I was in denial about what was going on, incompetent in a crisis situation, he would have to take charge himself*. Gradually, however, he began to catch on to the sinister undertone of my apparent apathy. Not that he understood the real reason for my behavior; but he understood, at least, that dealing with me directly would be futile. Infuriated by my calm indifference, he left, slamming the door behind him.

He must have gone straight to the police, as that evening I received my first *official* visit.

The man—by the time I responded to his incessant ringing he was already holding up his shield and smiling crookedly at me through the screen door—introduced himself as Detective Garibidian. He was sorry to bother me, he was just following up on a missing persons report filed on a Ms. Geary by our mutual friend, Gordon Glenn, he understood, of course, that for whatever reason I hadn't felt such a step necessary, that was a little strange, but seeing as how Ms. Geary and myself were not married (what this had to do with anything, I have no idea), he was obliged to act on Mr. Glenn's report, he just needed to ask me a few questions, he was sure it would come to nothing.

Stone faced—I was getting comfortable in my new persona, having had ample opportunity to practice on Gordon—I let the Detective in. I made the coffee again, this time choosing two of the daintiest cups I could find to serve it in. I offered one to the Detective, which he accepted without emotion and then set down on the table in front of him, ignoring it for the rest of the visit.

He was a huge man, broad and thick, with a head worthy of Rushmore. His trunk-like forearms bulged from his shirtsleeves and terminated in enormous hands with impossibly large fingers, all of which were essentially furred. Indeed, he was easily the hairiest human I had ever met. The hairline of his thick black hair could not have started more than an inch above his brow. He wore a heavy moustache and a beard that, despite the fact that he had probably shaved that morning, was already almost full. The relatively small patch of skin comprising his face seemed to be carved from the surrounding forest of black with a hammer and chisel. What's more, he was uncommonly fidgety for someone so large, his speech and manner riddled with tics.

With clear, precise body language, I shepherded him away from the inviting, oversized couch on the other side of the room and into a small wooden chair. Reluctantly, he wedged himself in, then sat quietly, hands resting tentatively on his knees, his eyes darting about the room in what at first seemed a caricature of studious observation. But then he turned to regard me, and his eyes kept dancing. I had seen this before. He was one of those people incapable of maintaining direct eye contact for more than a microsecond at a stretch. Perhaps out of sympathy, I too began to look away whenever our eyes accidentally aligned. An awkward, uncomfortable mood settled on the room, and the Detective actually began to look at me as if *I* were the shifty one.

Finally, perhaps as a way of breaking the silence, he repeated in an offhand manner that it was somewhat odd that Gordon, and not me, had filed the report.

I replied that unlike Gordon, I wasn't worried about Grace. Which didn't mean that I had any idea of her whereabouts. I had nothing to hide, I knew nothing. I didn't know any of Grace's relatives or even where she was from, for that matter. What little I did know, which was essentially personal, I felt no compulsion to share. As far as I was concerned, I told the bear/man stuffed into my rocking chair, this was a personal matter, not a police one.

Blinking furiously, he nodded his agreement with my assessment, even as he informed me that, in his unfortunately considerable experience with such things, all police matters inevitably evolve from personal ones.

I smiled crookedly in response to his platitude. He, in turn, ignored my expression. Stroking the long black caterpillar that was his eyebrow, he switched subjects, asking what efforts I had been making to locate Grace.

I told him that so far I had done nothing, apart from waiting, and that for now I had no intention of doing more. He winced painfully at my response, as if suddenly afflicted with a severe gastrointestinal cramp.

He took a few notes, asked a few more casual, innocent-sounding questions, and then pronounced our interview—his word for it—over. He left in a flurry of throat-clearings and strange clucks and half-hearted apologies.

Almost immediately, I began having second thoughts about my approach. I was being too passive, I thought, too robotic. My attitude, though derived from the truth, made me seem cold, calculating. I thought then of other things I could have shared with him, things I cold have volunteered, such as the motivation for my behavior. It was true that I didn't know anything. What I didn't feel like sharing was why it was that I didn't know anything. That, as I said, was personal.

For his part, I think Garibidian, as much to stave off boredom as anything, decided to see me as an enigma, a challenge, albeit a temporary one. He would assail my position—that I knew nothing, that Grace was not a victim of some treachery of mine—from every possible angle over the coming weeks. No one could accuse the man of a lack of diligence. But I never wavered. If anything, I just got better at the dissimulation, at playing the Detective's game well enough to keep him at bay. But as I had truly *done nothing*, he would get no nearer to implicating me than he had been when he first showed up at my door. More importantly, he would not get me to tell him about *us*.

I think only my fidelity to our private universe can explain my attitude in the face of these trying circumstances. It was if I thought that, by refusing to respond to Gordon's completely predictable efforts with anything other than bemused silence, by responding to the attempts of the police to bait me with smug indifference, by not doing exactly what was expected from someone in my situation, I was somehow being faithful to *us*, keeping *us* intact.

In a way, our life together was like a cat in one of those cartoons: we could walk across thin air, so long as we didn't look down, so long as we refused to acknowledge the established rules of perception and behavior that order the world around us. We had created a world apart, one with laws of our own devising. One that worked only so long as we were both there to keep it spinning.

It probably sounds strange, but this world was built, more than anything around silence. Not the silence of the secretive, or of people who have long since run out of things to say to each other. It had to do, rather, with our essential natures: Grace was a listener, I was a watcher. Silent activities.

It was due to this silence that we met. In a room full of talkers, it is inevitable that the listener and the watcher should recognize each other. Inevitable, in a *world* of talkers, that they should come together.

Over time, we sort of broadened each other's perceptual spectrum. She became a more keen visual observer of things, just as I came to listen more attentively, to *hear* things, to understand sounds as things in themselves.

We came to share a common perception, like twins. If we were together, we were sure to experience things in the same manner, things that were effectively invisible or inaudible to others. As we became more aware of this fact the silence grew. We did our best to act naturally—that is, artificially—in social situations, but I think we basically scared off most people. We probably got too comfortable in this mode, too confident in the belief that we were always thinking the same thing. And we refused to acknowledge the fact that silence could still harbor secrets, just as we refused to acknowledge anything that might have threatened our belief.

Like the past. Like talking.

That's my truth, our secret. We had a language of our own. A sign language. Not so deep, really. Probably not so strange, either. But, insignificant to the *case* as it might have been, I was not about to turn it over to Gordon or Garibidian or anyone else just so they would understand why I didn't know anything about why Grace was gone (not missing, as I kept telling Garibidian). Because I really didn't know *why*, because I didn't know anything about the person closest to me, didn't know her in any way apart from this idea of *us*. Because we had never bothered to ask, to confide in each other.

What we take for sight—not the mechanics of vision, but that which makes up our visual percepts—would of course be nothing without the other senses to bolster it. For a person endowed with vision, but deprived of smell and hearing and touch, the world would be little more than a vast *Quattrocento* composition, a hollow, lifeless world, without fluidity, each moment severed from the next, an endless cascade of geometric formalities.

But when you examine it more closely it's not obvious that perception can be so neatly apportioned into discrete senses. We think of a bright, lazy summer day, and the first thing that comes to mind is the familiar luminosity of a clear blue sky. But would that same day be recognizable as such without the feeling of being enveloped in a hum of warm air, or the barely felt passage of an innocuous breeze? Without a certain pungency in the air, redolent of grass clippings and hot pavement? Without the myriad sounds of birds and insects, of small airplanes Dopplering across the sky? Such a summer day, and in particular the memory of it, which will inform the perception of summer days to come, is no more or less encoded in one sense than another. They're intertwined, interdependent in a way, though I think each, if it had to, could still carry the bulk of the memory on its own.

Grace's recordings speak for this capability relative to hearing. You select a disc from her library entitled Summer and play it back, headphones on, eyes closed. You hear the plane motoring overhead, moving away from you left to right along a slow, soft angle. You *feel* again the delicate atmospheric conditions, *smell* the grass and the road kill. You *see* the sun reflecting off cars and houses, heat shimmering on the horizon, the endless blue sky.

Any recording she's made, of any object, on any subject, has this quality to it. It's like a form of time travel. I really don't know the first thing about the technical side of it, but I do know that even a lot of her colleagues don't know how she does it, especially as she has apparently remained pretty low-tech. Relatively speaking, of course. And she never involves herself in any project—most of which are Gordon's—beyond the field recordings. She just goes off and captures whatever he's looking for and hands it over, then moves on to something else. It's safe to say that Gordon would be a far less successful man without Grace. Which explains, at least in part, his *altruism*.

I've spent a lot of time in the studio over the last six weeks, listened to almost two years of Grace's work. Initially, I was listening, or so I thought, for some sort of clue. A destination call in an airport, an inadvertent confession, a snippet of threatening conversation, something like that. In reality, I sought something else: some sign of her presence. An exhalation, a quiet cough, clothes rustling, Grace talking to herself. For countless hours I listened, ears red and aching beneath the headphones, straining to make out the slightest sound that might betray her actually having been there, making the recording. But there was nothing. Dozens of projects, miles of DAT, hours of MiniDisc. Birds, wind, water, traffic, people, music, machines, trains, dying light bulbs, leaves falling. But no Grace.

Not one breath.

By the end of last week I had worked my way up to her most recent stuff, recordings of various playgrounds made over a month-long period. Incredible stuff, really. Sounds of merry-go-rounds and jungle gyms, games of four square and hopscotch. The voices of children, laughing, singing, screaming for each other's attention, devising arcane rules to *ad hoc* games. The feet of children, running over tan bark, sand, grass, blacktop. A schoolyard playground at recess; it could just as well have been the rookery of some species of raucous seabird.

The very last piece, the most recently recorded piece, was simply ten minutes of the repetitive, high-pitched drone of a swing. The swing itself was easy to picture: even lengths of metal chain suspended from a steel A-frame, hooked to a seat of India rubber, the manufacturer's stamp worn smooth through years of use. She had made the recording, it was clear, while sitting in that seat. While swinging.

After a minute or two of listening, I could actually feel it, could feel myself in the swing, moving back and forth, feel the momentary sensation of weightlessness in my gut at the zenith of each swing, feel myself being slowly hypnotized by the rhythmic chant of the last link of chain squeaking in its metal housing.

It was a childhood spell, the kind that abolishes the passage of time. An ideal moment, extended indefinitely through perfect repetition. And she had captured it.

Back in the studio, I played the disc that had arrived that morning. Initially, it appeared I was right in assuming it belonged with the current project. It *was* a recording of a playground. It started out innocently enough, a mix of sounds familiar to me by now from the others. Maybe she had simply gone to a place she remembered that had an object with some unique sound quality that she *had* to get for the project (though I knew this could not possibly take six weeks).

In any event, the disc itself cut short my train of thought.

After a couple of minutes of standard park sounds, it too came to a swing segment. It was uncanny, really. The same swing, sing virtually the same song. But somehow subtly different. I don't know how she did it, but she had recorded the swing in Forest Lawn playground—I had to assume it was from there—in such a way that behind its sing-song one felt the presence of something ominous, foreboding. Before I could put my finger on the source of this threat, the swing gave way to the sound of traffic. No angry honking of horns or squealing of tires, just the cumulative threat of violence and destruction lurking in the belly of so many powerful machines. Then the sound of traffic was cut short and replaced by a high pitched scream, more of a squeal, really, whether from terror or just mere surprise I couldn't tell. Slowly, the scream trailed off into silence.

I pulled headphones off and leaned back in Grace's task chair, staring at the ceiling absently.

My heart was pounding.

This wasn't simply a message from the past. It was a plea or a summons. Or a confession. Not that it mattered precisely which. It was enough, whatever it was, to break through the impasse of the last six weeks. I realized, finally, that the only us was the one we had constructed, one which was ultimately just a barrier to our ever really knowing the *other*. One that had allowed me to sit here for six weeks.

I hadn't done anything to speak of, just played one MiniDisc, but I was exhausted. I grabbed a blanket and went to sleep on the studio's second-hand couch.

I was startled awake by the phone ringing. My first thought, as always, was to let the call go to voice mail. But then I thought it might be Grace, so I picked it up, just after the fourth ring.

I waited.

There was a faint tapping sound, as if the person at the other end was drumming his fingers on the edge of the speaker. It had to be Garibidian. This was part of a game we had developed over the past few weeks, seeing who could most annoy the other.

I kept waiting.

Finally, "Mr. Glynn?" It was indeed Garibidian, his voice heavy with apparent disinterest.

I countered his opening gambit with pure vacancy.

"Yes."

A brief silence. I knew the giant, shaggy head at the other end of the line would already be shaking with mildly amused chagrin.

"This is Detective Garibidian, Mr. Glynn."

A short breath, followed by a woeful exhalation.

"Anything *new* to tell me? Have you heard anything concerning *Ms.* Geary?"

A soft clucking sound.

"Shouldn't I be asking you that?"

"Yes, quite right. Heard anything *from* her, I should say?" A dry sniff. "But we both know you won't, so I'm taking the liberty of doing it for you."

More clucking.

"No, nothing new. Mmmmmm. Well, actually, yes. There is something. I got a message from her this morning."

"She called you? You spoke with her?"

There was a meaningful absence of contrived noises.

"No, I didn't speak with her. She sent me a package."

"But you're sure it's from her?"

I *tsked* like a disapproving Grandmother. "I'm not completely without deductive skills, *Garibidian*."

"Of course you're not."

He whistled softly under his breath.

"Well, okay, what was *in* the package, then, Mr. Glynn?"

"Well, I don't know," I lied, yawning. I wasn't ready to share the disc and its contents with him just yet. "As a matter of fact, I was on my way to open the package when you inter—when you called. But I can assure you that she's fine, she's safe. At least in the ways that matter to your *investigation*."

"Well okay, Mr. Glynn, that's good news. I assume you'll have no objections to my dropping by a little later then, just to check the contents of this package for myself, assure *myself* of her well-being?"

He waited, humming

"No. No objection."

"Good. As long as I'm satisfied that the package constitutes a reasonable proof of her well-being and whereabouts, then we can bring this thing to a close. Or at least *my* investigation. And you can get on with your life."

I would have liked nothing better than for Garibidian to be able to close the book on the case in good conscience. But for some reason, I couldn't see him interpreting the contents of the disc in the same manner as myself. If I let him listen to it, I knew, things would only get more complicated, at least for a while.

I could hear him flicking the tip of his tongue happily back and forth across his lower lip as he awaited my response.

"Fine. I look forward to it. Goodbye, Garibidian."

"You take care of yourself, Mr. Glynn."

In the end, there was less effort involved in getting to the bottom, or at least near the bottom, of the *mystery* then there had been in simply working up the nerve to play the disc. I left the envelope and the labeled disc case in the mailbox for Garibidian, along with a brief note explaining my intentions. I kept the disc for myself. As a formality, I also left him a number for my mobile phone, even though I don't have one.

I rented a car and drove up to Graeburn, with the hope of establishing Grace's presence there, either now or at some point in the past.

It was a long drive, taking up the better part of a day, a potentially unfortunate fact that I turned to my advantage by stopping, on more than one occasion, at certain roadside diner franchises. It was early evening when, literally brimming with the remnants of my last meal—meatloaf, fries, a watery milk shake and a slice of key lime pie—I pulled into Graeburn.

Graeburn is a quintessential baby boom town, with the standard cluster of euphemistically named subdivisions, organized around parks and ball fields, with a few broad avenues, cul-de-sacs and dead ends to offset the otherwise limited diversity of building materials and floor plans. The buildings—from the houses and schools to the small, prototypical shopping malls—were vintage late-fifties architecture, flat, expansive structures that belied a misplaced faith in manifest destiny. Probably by design, there was no trace of the traditional American downtown.

But the town's heyday, which most likely only ever existed in the imagination anyway, had long since come and gone, and I saw more than one school with boarded up windows, another that had been converted into a college of chiropractic. Even the town's boundaries were uncertain, surrounded now by a nebulous margin of U-Stor-It warehouses and office parks.

Ironically enough, the town's most striking feature was its trees. Full, mature maples and oaks, towering beech and cedars. Most likely scrawny saplings and juvenile transplants at the town's inception, they had grown into venerable and beautiful souls, even as the houses and buildings to which they were chained slipped from planned uniformity into baroque decay. I drove around for a while, touring the town, before taking a room in a motel on its outskirts. I settled in and tried to figure out what I was going to do next.

I'm no detective. And my contact with Garibidian hadn't exactly left me full of insight into the art of solving of mysteries. On the road, I had envisioned myself walking assuredly into something called *The Hall of Records* and finding everything I would need in a folder labeled *Grace Geary*. And yet, once there, I realized that I couldn't even be certain that Geary was her last name, that she hadn't changed it, shed it along with the rest of her past. Indeed, I was taking a huge leap in assuming that she was even *from* Graeburn.

I ended up taking a rather dilettantish tack. I drove to the high school and slipped into the library. Once inside, I looked up the yearbooks from the period when Grace would have been enrolled, as well as the years book-ending this time. My theory was that by finding her picture I would establish that she *had* lived there, at least through her teenage years, and could work my way back from there. But I found nothing. Maybe she went to a private high school, though that was doubtful. This didn't seem to be the kind of town that had those. Acknowledging that it was a stupid approach, I hurried out of the library, choosing instead to cruise the town in search of lunch.

Full stomach, clear head. After lunch I adopted a more direct approach. I located the nearest library branch and searched the microfiche archive of the local newspaper, starting, naturally, with April 19, 1972.

The pages of the *Graeburn Daily Review*, like most of those printed in 1972, were filled with names which, as I had first I encountered them at the tender age of six, still resonated with quasi-mythological meaning: Nixon, G. Gordon Liddy, Johns Dean and Mitchell, Watergate. Resisting the allure of these ultimately irrelevant time capsules as best as possible, I eventually came across an article in the *Local Times* section, from April 20. The article left little doubt that I had found what I was looking for:

Graeburn Boy in Fatal Playground Mishap
Staff – A boy was struck and killed by an automobile yesterday afternoon, near the intersection of Forest Lawn Avenue and Keller Street. Timothy Flanagan, five, of Graeburn, was leaving the Forest Lawn Park playground

with his older brother when he was struck while attempting to cross the street. According to witnesses, Flanagan darted into the street from between two parked cars, and was probably not even seen by the oncoming vehicle. According to Deputy Sheriff Gus Gasey, the driver of the vehicle, 32 year-old Gilbert Geary, also of Graeburn, was on his way to pick up his daughter, who was also at the playground at the time. Gasey indicated that no criminal charges are foreseen. "It's an unfortunate situation, really, just a . . ."

I searched ahead a few more weeks, but found no further mention of the incident, apart from a funeral notice for Timothy Flanagan.

The obviousness of it was almost cartoonish. Timothy Flanagan. T.F. Killed at the Forest Lawn playground on April 19, 1972, by Grace's father.

It was four o'clock. Late afternoon sun streamed through the library's water stained windows and glared off the microfiche view screen. I left the library and drove around aimlessly, crisscrossing the town. Inevitably, my meandering brought me to Forest Lawn Park.

It was a study in suburban decomposition. The park itself occupied about an acre and a half of patchy grass. The lawn was etched with numerous dusty footpaths, where people had been too lazy to stick to the paved walkway that bisected the park, and bordered by row of forlorn trees, the roots of which were exposed and scarred. A shallow cement wading pool, with a defunct, sand-clogged fountain, was set in the center of the lawn, and now held only cigarette butts and other scraps of litter. The pool was ringed by several pre-cast concrete benches, of a style that one might mistakenly have called *Utopian*, their once smooth surfaces now chipped and jagged, tagged with redundant layers of artless graffiti. A few of these benches faced away from the pool and toward the skeletal remains of the playground, which was adjacent to it. Steel climbing apparatus, death traps by today's overzealous standards, were set amidst a bed of moldering and disintegrated tan bark. From a long, rickety metal frame that could easily have held eight swings, only two remained, hanging unevenly.

The park was completely deserted.

I found the swing with the familiar squeak and sat in it. I swung joylessly for a couple of minutes, then took one of Grace's portable MiniDisc players and some headphones from my coat pocket. I put the phones on and inserted the disc. I pressed PLAY and closed my eyes, still swinging.

I listened to the disc again and again. At length I came to know—or at least I *believe* I came to know—what happened on that day in 1972. I'm not saying that I had a vision or anything, that I knew what happened exactly the way it happened. In the end, I'm just guessing. But I'm sure my guess is not all that far from the truth, and that's enough for me.

Grace is swinging in this very same swing, waiting for her father to pick her up. Just swinging, toes pointed first to the sky, then pulled quickly back beneath her seat, she's climbing ever higher, if you let her she'd swing for hours. She's composing the rhyming words to a song as she swings, something to match the rhythm of the squeaking chain. Then she sees her father's car, a shiny blue sedan, turn the corner and head along the street in front of the park. He's looking over toward the playground, through the passenger side window, he sees her and waves, leaning now across the passenger seat. A smile spreads across her face, she pulls one hand from the chain to wave back, but it never gets there, it goes to her face instead, because she sees him, sees Timmy Flanagan run out into the road, in front of her father's shiny blue car. There's no sound of skidding, nobody yells, nobody sees him but her. Then the car, which hasn't slowed at all, hits him, and there's a sound that cannot be described. *He flies through the air*, she can't believe how far he flies, and lands on the front lawn of a neighboring house. Only then, after he has hit the ground, does she scream. She finds her voice again, too late.

Her father, according to my version, is never the same after that. He becomes sullen, withdrawn, gray. Every once in while, an unprovoked fit of rage bursts through the silence, but then even this rage, which at least exposed the presence of a person, recedes, and he's gone again. They lose friends, Graeburn isn't home anymore, they move to another town, then another, never staying in one place for more than a couple years. Eventually, everyone forgets why it's like this, forgets all about the accidental death of Timothy Flanagan, the accidental death of a family.

For years, before she manages to forget, at the point in Grace's memory where the indescribable sound of that impact should have been, there is instead only a void, a deep, soundless black.

Eventually, when she's is old enough, she leaves it all behind. She, too, never stops. She just keeps going forward, in order to keep it all forgotten. When she does pause, it's only to capture a sound, imprison a sound in a little plastic case, then store it safely away in the old shed out in the yard.

~

It's been hours—and maybe two-hundred miles—since I watched the last of Graeburn's office parks shrink to a speck and then disappear from the rear-view mirror, and I haven't stopped once. Not even to answer the Siren call of the waffle house. *Loss of appetite*, I think it's called.

At best, I'm four days behind Grace.

But there's something strange about being out here in the middle of nowhere—or the middle of somewhere, from most people's perspective. From here, four days in any direction somehow seems closer than home. I look over at the passenger seat, where the road map—having foiled my every attempt to refold it properly—lies crumpled in a ball.

mist

> *But if they were not used to swerve, all things would fall downwards through the void like drops of rain, nor could collision come to be, nor a blow brought to pass for the first beginnings.*
>
> - Lucretius

SHE STARES OUT from her second-floor window, listening to the clock but not yet prepared to look at it. *I need to leave*, she thinks. *But not just yet.*

The window frames the same scene as always: the upper stories and rooftops of the drab houses across the way, angled chimneys reflecting the unobserved process of settlement and decay; the verdant row of mature oaks just beyond the houses, forming an uneven band of green above the dull gray and black rooftops; the tendrilled branch-work of an adolescent willow, spilling over the window's right edge, the rest of the tree set somewhere wide of her view and therefore non-existent; the power lines and telephone wires, traversing the pane at soft angles. All else is sky, a uniform shade of gray, the kind of sky from which rain threatens, but never falls.

Against the dark green of random foliage and the black of vacant windows, an incredibly fine mist can be just barely discerned. The mist is so soft that it is at first indistinguishable from that point where vision, lacking a suitable object, breaks down and turns on itself, the limit of perception becoming somehow perceptible, an infinite field of dots and spots and transient colors. The air being otherwise completely still, the mist falls earthward without the slightest obstruction, heavy and slow.

For a moment, even though she already knows it won't last, she feels it: new constants, new limits with their attendant hierarchies, have been introduced into the physical universe, displacing the mathematical hegemony of gravity and the electromagnetic field.

This is her world. Closer, heavier, and much, much slower; it barely moves. *It's because of the mist*, she thinks. *It's steady and uniform, it fills space and so banishes time.*

She inhales deeply, then lets her breath out slowly. A creator's breath. Her shoulders rise, straighten. She opens the window with the tip of her finger, effortlessly. Kneeling, she rests her head on the sill, letting her arm dangle from the open window. Gradually, the skin and fine hairs of her arm become attuned, like her eyes, to the impossibly delicate mist falling upon them.

I need to leave, she thinks. *But not just yet.*

Her eyes closed, she welcomes each atom of mist, the elementary particles of her universe, to her cheek.

She waits.

the not perfectly spherical object

DREAMING, IN THE FINAL MOMENTS ALLOTTED TO SLEEP. I'm seated at the counter of a nearly empty soda fountain with two others, a man and a woman, both some years younger than myself and quite attractive, sporting the latest hairstyles and eyewear. They are delta-wave acquaintances, appearing in my dreams quite often but in reality unknown to me.

We sit quietly, eyes fixed on the orange countertop in front of us, our forearms resting in depressions worn into the ancient surface by the innumerable others that have come before us. Our silence and slumped shoulders suggest the hungry somnolence of weary travelers.

Although it would be logical to assume that we are eagerly awaiting the arrival of our food, that we exist for no other purpose than this waiting, such is not the case. Instead of the usual diner fare, we have ordered a TV and VCR.

The service doors swing open and our waitress emerges from the infernal din of the kitchen with our order, the television adroitly balanced on her right hip, the VCR wedged in the crook of her left arm. The inside joke that is her identity finally dawns on us and we share a wry, knowing glance. Our waitress—peach smock, white apron, paper bonnet and all—is William F. Buckley Jr.

Favoring us with an occasional furtive scowl but otherwise pointedly ignoring us, Buckley deposits the TV on the counter, setting the VCR beside it. She quickly connects the two, plugs them into an electrical outlet set into the counter, then pulls a universal remote from her apron. Leaning over the counter, she aims the remote at the devices and, from a distance of a few inches, turns them on. As with most VCRs, the clock on ours begins to blink. It flashes: REPENT.

With a whoosh of the double doors, Buckley is reabsorbed into the kitchen. The young man reaches into his bike messenger bag and pulls out a video tape. It's a copy of the new, as yet unreleased, David Lynch film. The dreaming-me finds nothing unusual in this, having also attended diner screenings of *Wild At Heart* and *Lost Highway* well before they were released, or even filmed.

My young acquaintance puts the tape into the VCR. The lights in the diner dim, the film begins.

Although the opening titles (the film is called *Short Session*) are for the most part unremarkable, the three of us are quite taken with the mysterious quality of the film itself. It has a blemishy, metallic feel, as if shot in Daguerreotype. The young woman inquires about the film stock. Eager to prove my worth to my young acquaintances, who are clearly quite knowledgeable on matters of cinema, I struggle to come up with the answer. I'm on the verge of fabricating one when the young man says, in an irritated, offhand way, "Tschervinsky." The woman nods as if this answer merely provided confirmation of her own suspicion. We fall silent and turn our attention back to the film.

The opening sequence, a night scene, is a clever and disorienting series of directional transfers. A steam locomotive barrels down a set of tracks, heading east. The camera tracks the train until it passes beneath a roadway, where it picks up a black sedan, speeding north. The car is followed in turn until it hurtles past a long haul tractor-trailer—the kind with three trailers, like you see in Utah or Colorado—heading in the opposite direction. The camera jumps to the truck, staying with it until it comes to a rural airfield, where a light aircraft is taking off from a dirt runway perpendicular to the interstate. The point of view transfers to the plane, its laborious ascent followed patiently by the camera.

Buffeted by turbulence, the plane bounces about the frame, producing a subtle hallucinatory effect: it begins to look like a toy. I've already succumbed to the skeptical compulsion to search for hidden wires when, quite unexpectedly, the passenger-side door opens and a spherical object is tossed from the plane.

We witness the free-fall of the spherical object through the void. Whitish, turning slow revolutions as it falls, the object stands in stark contrast to a featureless background of pure black. Despite being presented in extreme slow motion, the object remains blurry and indistinct. For the duration of its descent, the film is silent.

Then the spherical object crashes to earth in an explosion of primordial sound and dust. The cloud expands, billowing fractally across the screen, then begins to settle.

The Badalamenti score kicks in.

At the precise moment when the cloud has dissipated enough to reveal the grainy presence of the object, the object itself begins rolling.

Apparently not perfectly spherical, it wobbles and bounces down a dirt hillock adjacent to a deserted country road and into the makeshift campsite of a pair of vagabonds, played by Lynch regulars Freddie Jones and Jack Nance.

Eventually, the object comes to rest at the feet of one of the vagabonds (Jones), seated on a wooden crate in front of the fire, hugging his knees to his chest and rocking back and forth. That he has taken note of the sudden manifestation of the object can be inferred only by the increased tempo of his rocking and the onset of a pronounced, Tourette-ish ear tugging.

His cohort (Nance), who had been standing off to one side with his arms crossed, looking into the night, now turns to regard the object. His soiled, screwed-up face displays a mix of amusement, thoughtfulness, and that perpetually simmering rage common to the psychotic. Deeply paranoid, he's not surprised by the object's arrival; he seems, almost, to have expected it. His contorted expression mirrors an inner despair: *Will they pursue me to the ends of the earth!?*

Walking over to the object with an awkward, shuffling gait, he nudges it with the toe of his tape-encased shoe. His socks are white. He chews at the inside of his lower lip.

At length he reaches down and picks up the object, if only to bring it into plain view of the camera. The object, like his face, glows dull orange in the firelight.

Predictably enough, the strange semi-spherical object is revealed to be a charred human head, capped with a pair of white Y-front men's briefs. Long strands of wispy black hair sprout from the leg holes. The Nance character holds the head by these strands, one in each hand. It swings gently back and forth, the blackened face moving in and out of the orange light. He brings the head close to his face, staring at it menacingly with one eye, squinting the other like Popeye. The lush, portentous score softens for a moment, allowing us to hear his heavy breathing. He yells at the head, "Get A Job!!!" Then, his voice falling to a whisper this time, "Get a job."

Nance glances meaningfully at the fire, which does not, as a fire should, crackle or sputter. It throbs ominously with chthonic foreboding. His eyes widen momentarily, signaling the reception of a divine communiqué, then he resumes his scrutiny of the head. He laughs, the standard actor's approximation of a deranged vagabond laugh, then tosses the head onto the fire. The flames flare up violently with the addition of this uncanny fuel. The screen is engulfed in a blaze of yellow-orange, then goes black, silent.

The film is over.

There is the most obligatory of pauses, after which my young acquaintances and I launch into an earnest post-film critique. Lynch is duly praised. The young man harps on his unparalleled sense of style, his *near absolute* mastery of the arcane. The young woman, as if determined to make up for the weakness exposed by her earlier question, gushes over Lynch's utterly maverick utilization of Tschervinsky, which, *as everyone knows*, is temperamental at best. After making this point two or three times, she adds her admiration for Lynch's ability to evoke a world that, despite being populated only by machines and clichéd hobos, remains undeniably erotic.

I more than hold my own during this *discussion*, pointing out how Lynch's deft employment of the short form allows him to more forcefully drive home his point, and marveling at the technical acumen required in shooting the entire film in one take. Still, I feel compelled to have the last word. Tossing it off as if it were almost too obvious to mention, I remark on Lynch's clever use of the fact that I'm dreaming.

They turn on me immediately, the young man blurting out, "Yes, *that's right*, you don't even wear Y-fronts, do you? I'll bet you don't even . . ." while the young woman, with an irritated toss of her hair, barks, "Unbelievable! I mean, what typical Aristotelian bla . . ."

The faces of my acquaintances go suddenly blank, their rants left unfinished. Staring straight ahead with a strangely vacant malevolence, they raise their right arms and point at me. Then, like agitated body snatchers, they begin screeching, repeatedly and in unison, "Re-Pent, Re-Pent, Re-Pent . . ."

Gradually, their horrible, shrieking admonition merges with, then becomes, the piercing digital klaxon of my alarm clock. Still deeply fatigued, unable, even, to open my eyes, I grope for the button that will make it stop.

phthalo blue

(for Bob Ross, in memoriam)

AND THEN BOB SAYS:
May-be . . . maybe another tree lives here, right next to our big willow . . . maybe a little tree this time . . . you decide. Maybe a whole family of willows lives right here, right alongside our little stream . . . it's your world, you decide . . .

And I think: I'd rather not.

Much more satisfying just to lay here, listening to the softly spoken words, watching—beholding, as they used to say—the magical appearance of mossy stones and puffy clouds and babbling brooks. So much easier to be reminded of my freedom, of the power of art lying in my soul too, than to decide, to move.

Bob conjures the little tree, its trunk Van Dyke Brown mixed with Yellow Ochre, the shaggy bough Phthalo Green, Indian Yellow and Titanium White, in less than a minute. He places it beside the fatherly willow. Another tree follows just as swiftly, bigger this time though not quite as tall as the first. And there it is, just like that, a happy family of willows, living beside a cool, clear stream, a wet on wet idyll.

As always in these moments of completion, I feel a deep calm descend upon me, even as the familiar heaviness, the burden of intelligent matter tethered to space and time, lifts, rising from somewhere in my chest and drifting away. I close my eyes.

This arrangement is best. Bob decides. I watch.

. . . and up here in the sky, maybe the storm has just passed, and maybe there's a little bit of white cloud mixed in with the gray . . . and maybe, over here, we can see some blue sky, just a little bit, peeking through . . .

The curtains are all drawn, a cheap magic protecting me from the sooty gray sky outside, from the leafless branches of dormant trees, from the utility poles, leaning beneath the weight of transformers and an ever-growing tangle of cables and boxes, from the inert watchfulness of the neighboring homes, with their eerie conglomerations of do-it-yourself improvements, from the dampened asphalt's oily rainbows and the uneven concrete walks, freckled with blackened chewing gum.

I understand the necessity of all this, of course. The cable that runs from the pole across the street to the side of my building, for example, delivering to my television the peaceful images that alone make the pole bearable in the first place.

It's midday, not that you'd know it in the artificial dusk of my apartment. I'm lying on the couch, wearing only a robe, and socks. I understand the necessity of this costume, too, recognize in it the truth of my viewing habits: the dovetailing of a vacant, effortless voyeurism and a congenitally inclined onanism.

I inhale the stale air of my living room as deeply as I can, then breath it all out. I do this a few times, sifting an all-encompassing numbness—seriously, it penetrates to the very core of my being—for its constituent parts, trying, as always, to establish a fair and accurate distribution of symptoms. What portion of this numbness, I wonder, can be written off as mere physical background noise, the distant complaint of unused muscles, hovering on the threshold of atrophy, and what can be ascribed to so-called *anxiety*. And what share of this anxiety, I ask myself, should be chalked up to things beyond my control—the gradual diminution of the polar ice caps, for example, or the sinister ubiquity of microbes, or *Jihad*. And then, how much of this *anxious numbness* is indigenous, the product, perhaps, of vile humors and malignant brain juices, of the biological foundations of denial (what could possibly be the use, after all, of a creature that is *honest with itself*, what evolutionary advantage could the acts of confession and penance possibly confer?). My analysis never gets past this first step. Invariably, it ends up awash in the oxbows of thought. So, over time, I've reached something of a compromise. I demand of myself, of the *numbness*, but one personal truth a day. The rest I dismiss as the anxiety of a being evolved to be anxious.

. . . and maybe rays of sunlight break through the clouds . . . right over here . . . and maybe, maybe they shine right on our little meadow, right in the middle . . . you decide, it's your world, and in your world you can do whatever you want . . . you decide . . .

My gaze directs itself—it doesn't seem to be *me* who does it—toward this new marvel, ethereal streaks of Cadmium Yellow and Titanium White, like the light of Angels, shooting down from the clouds and touching the earth. Bob keeps talking—*that soothing voice!*—and painting, and cleaning brushes with vigor. And in this moment, brief as it is, this so-called *window of time*, a kind of equilibrium is established between my self and the space in which it happens to be situated. Not a balance between dynamically opposed forces, but a merging of those forces, a dissolution of their supposed antinomy. It's like the famous One of Parmenides, the atomless plenum of Being breaching and permeating the artificial boundaries of skin and ego. It turns out Parmenides was talking about a kind of hum, a hum that can occasionally be felt above the *anxious numbness*.

It's a momentary thing, this cosmic union. It gradually gives way to a faint tingling in my extremities, the hum becoming a buzz and then a palpitation. I roll onto my side, pulling my knees up closer to my chest, and move my cold hands between my thighs. For warmth, of course, but not only that.

~

... and that's the beautiful thing about art, the power is all yours. In the world of art, you decide what goes in your painting, your world, you make the beauty, you decide ...

On the couch in semi-darkness again. Again, with the robe; and the same socks, I think. Undoubtedly, there are pills for this. Pills that bisect this vicious circle, a socially inappropriate mixture of cholines and amines, bad brain chemistry begetting the fear and unease that begets even worse brain chemistry.

And maybe, with these pills, I could go outside and see, instead of besotted pavement and pinched, evil faces, the world a giant glass ashtray, everything coated in a strange distorting film, maybe I would see instead a fanciful but not too deceptive *trompe l'oeil* of Midnight Black and Gesso Gray and Liquid Opal, of Alizarin Crimson and Dark Sienna and Burnt Umber.

I have a theory on this question of pills. As I see it, it's really a question of decision. Or of changing the decision that's been made for you. A decision between the human brain—a mere lump of matter—on the one hand, and the mind—the ineffable excess of that lump—on the other. Not that I actually believe the distinction between the two to be this clear cut. I like to think of a brain/mind spectrum, a continuum wherein some degree of brain, however small, always mingles with mind, and vice versa. So the question of pills is a question of deciding where you reside on this hypothetical spectrum, which has been in place, unchanged, throughout history.

For surely there were poets and technicians and go-getters even among the Neanderthals, just as there are, in today's world, any number of cavemen. People like me. We can be found here, lying on our couches in darkened rooms, contemplating our numbness.

The pills, then, are for us cave dwellers.

... [...] ...

Bob is gone for the day, followed by what is apparently a children's program. Androgynous, mouthless beings awaken from a dreamless slumber inside some sort of sod covered tumulus and patter happily outside. They receive an invisible transmission aimed at the fleshy antennas sprouting from their heads. The message—I've turned down the volume so I can only guess at its contents, probably a song about the sun or a friendly reminder to always pick up after yourself—must be benign, because the smooth, sexless creatures respond to it with something like joy, hopping and skipping about, their stubby arms—useless for anything apart from waving—drawing random, excited circles in the air.

It's strange, now that I think about it, how I had the energy to turn off the sound but not the power. That's the allure of television, I suppose; it's easier to watch than not, easier even than sleeping. Another example: my robe is lying open, and I have the energy to avoid looking at myself, but not to pull the robe closed.

My left foot has gone cold, the sock which once covered it now lying on the floor beside the couch. I'm breathing in and out. This is my daily calisthenics, deep breathing and sorting out the numb, attempting to divvy it up, according to category, into various piles. And as for the *daily truth*: today, I manage to acknowledge the possibility that some of this unease could very well be a function of my erotic attachment to a television painting show.

It's not simply a question of an infatuation with Bob, though that's obviously part of it: the casual clothing, snug on his ascetic frame; the saintly nimbus of soft yet firmly permed hair; the sure hands, always spotless, gathering and mixing the colors, applying the paint with such ease that it seems as if the landscapes are revealed not so much through the act of painting as by the washing away of the blank canvas; the thoroughly charming compulsions exposed by certain thematic tendencies (over populating compositions with families of trees, for example); the soft reassuring voice, overflowing the television and bathing the room in concentric waves of calm.

So I'll not deny that Bob's something of a focal point, a flint for the sparking of Eros. But my investment in the show has as much to do with the paintings, *works of art* to which, if Bob is to be believed (and has there ever been anyone more trustworthy?) any one of us could give birth. Honestly, if I were forced to spend eternity imprisoned in one changeless moment, allowed to choose my own eternal prison, the scene of that prison would be one of Bob's paintings. Any one would do. An alpine meadow in spring, the mountains in the background topped by perennial snow caps. A clear mountain lake in summer, its still surface reflecting the blue sky and white clouds above and a family of pines by the shore. A sturdy lighthouse perched atop a rocky sea cliff, indifferent to the salty spray of the stormy surf.

But it's just more pointless fantasizing. We are not, of course, allowed to choose our prisons.

Somewhere, if not here than surely in Germany or Holland, someone makes pills for this. Nothing drastic, not some chemical lobotomy or something that only engenders, pharmacologically, additional layers of numbness. A pill, rather, to make me feel drug free. Just a little psychotropic nudge, a behavioral course correction, something that would aim me outward, give me a gentle push through the door. I'd leave the couch behind, take a little walk in the park, maybe become erotically attached to a person. From a distance, of course, but certainly a step in the right direction.

But in the end, I can't even contrive a scenario in wherein someone goes out and gets the pills on my behalf. Today's dose of truth: I believe the question of pills, of the brain/mind spectrum, doesn't apply to me. I'm actually too far down on the brain-heavy band for pills to be of any help. When it comes right down to it, I'm even less than a caveman—I spend more time horizontal than upright. My destiny lies not in the future but in the earth. And it's the earth that weighs on me, pulling me down, through the couch.

. . . and maybe, sitting here in our snow covered meadow, right next to the edge of the frozen pond but not too close, there's a little cabin. A cozy little cabin, maybe with some snow on the roof . . . ri-ght . . . there! And maybe there's a warm fire inside, and there's a little bit of smoke coming out of our chimney, right . . . over . . . here . . .

There's an immediate sense of foreboding, a signal flare from the watch tower, a warning call from the sentry. But something, the same thing that is trying to warn me—this is the kind of game it plays—turns my head toward the screen and has me watch.

Not that I need to see the painting, sitting there on the easel, Bob standing beside it and smiling proudly, giant kidney shaped palette resting weightless on his left forearm. He's not proud for himself, of course, he could do this painting blindfolded; he's proud for those of us out here who have just made one too. It's not that I need to see this painting to know what it looks like. I know exactly what the little cabin looks like. And the snow covered meadow, and the frozen pond. I've been there.

I'm crouching beside the frozen pond. I can do this, crouch, for hours without a loss of circulation, without my legs going numb, without the dizziness that accompanies standing up again. I'm crouching beside the frozen pond, most of which is covered with fresh snow. I'm right at the edge, I might even be on the pond itself, with all the snow it's not clear where the meadow ends and the pond begins. But it's been frozen solid for weeks, there's no danger of my crashing through. I've cleared away the snow in front of me with my heavy mittens, scraped and shoveled and swept aside six inches, maybe, from the icy surface. I'm a solitary snow creature, crouching beside a frozen sea in an arctic wilderness, working my way through enormous drifts with my snow claws.

I look down into the ice. It's clear enough, but not smooth. It's bumpy and wavy and just a little bit opaque, like my grandmother's kirsch bottle. I look down into the ice, and something's moving. A moment of shock, of terror almost, and then: It's a fish! There's a fish swimming beneath the ice, probably a trout. It's alive and not frozen solid, there's probably a whole other world down there, beneath the ice, and no one knows! Still crouching, I turn around to call up to the cabin, to yell for my grandmother to come and share my discovery, this portal to an impossible world. But she's already coming, stomping through the ankle deep snow. She's at my side. I begin telling her about the fish when she leans down, almost falling on top of me, and brings her face close to mine. Through clenched teeth, her real teeth, big as thighbones, she sputters: GOTT-DAIMED LITTLE BRAT. I SAID COME TO DIE HÜTTE FIVE MINUTES AGO!!!

That's her Teutonic gift to me, my guardian: *Gott-daimed.* No Liebchen, no Kleine Herr, no fresh-baked Linzer. *Gott-daimed.* That's what I got from her. Misplaced words, curses in an old world accent that I couldn't help but laugh at even as a large, spotted hand—the most basic of farm implements, handed down by generation upon generation of soil tillers, pig farmers, peasants—gropes for my ear, and I'm pulled to my feet by thick fleshy fingers with broad hard nails.

Once on my feet she jerks me forward by the elbow, it's mostly winter coat she's got hold of, but she's also pinching skin and flesh in the vise of her 19TH century hand. She pulls me along, full speed, she's practically dragging me up the path. And as I run-stumble to keep up—the realm of the intrepid, clawed snow creature and the hidden world beneath the ice already pushed far from consciousness and beyond recall—I can see the cabin, *die Hütte!,* over her shoulder. It sits on a small rise in the snow covered meadow, the corrugated metal roof also covered with snow, a thin column of gray smoke rising from the chimney and trailing off into the white winter sky.

. . . and maybe, in our world, the snow is falling again, big flakes and little flakes, a whole family of snowflakes, drifting slowly from the sky . . . just . . . like . . . so . . .

My body is limp and heavy, like I'm undergoing that form of public execution where they lay a door on top of you and then slowly pile the door with fist-sized rocks. I shut my eyes tight and resume breathing. After a time, I raise my hands to my eyes, pressing my thumbs against the lids. I used to do this long ago, tucked away for the night but unable to sleep, and then convince myself that I could see things in the powdery dance of phosphenes: polar bears, single-celled flagellates, individual atoms. And after all the years, the same colors are still here, inside. Subdued, chalky colors, like in the infrared. But I no longer see those magical forms. I find I can make out little more than a few orange-pink circles, and perhaps a field of swimming pinholes of the faintest red. It's a kaleidoscope without order, repetition or regularity. There's no pattern or image or representation. Not a single recognizable product of the mind. Beneath the lids it's just a roiling chaos.

They must have pills for this.

habitat

Donnie: Why do you wear that stupid bunny suit?
Frank: Why do you wear that stupid man suit?

- Donnie Darko

THEY'VE TAKEN ME TO THE ZOO AGAIN, even though I hate the zoo, even though nothing so thoroughly crushes my spirit like a trip to the zoo.

That it's not possible for a child to dislike the zoo; that, were it not for the frequent exposure to the catalyzing whiff of taxonomy afforded by these repeated trips to the zoo, I would be rendered incapable of synthesizing some essential cultural protein; that solely by dint of this exposure they are fulfilling their parental obligations (they're going *above and beyond*, really); that these repeated trips to the zoo are in no way related to the fact that they can think of nothing else to do with me. Having convinced themselves of all this, it's only natural that they should fail to notice the deep depression into which I always fall during these trips to the zoo, or how, afterwards, it always takes me days to emerge from the profound mental and physical torpor into which, on account of these trips, I am cast.

These days, at least, I come armed with a plan. Once inside the wrought iron gates, I run ahead, as if unable to constrain my enthusiasm, let the ambling crowd drift between us, leave the two of them behind. I find a bench, somewhere out of the way, one that looks on a well-formed tree or a nicely manicured spot of park. I remain on this bench for a period of time equivalent to the typical duration of our visits. To pass the time, I make up lists: famous historical figures who would have made more suitable parents; all the foods that make me gag at the thought of swallowing them; the number of women passing by with no discernible ankles. When it's time to go, I rejoin them—they'll be in front of the lion cage, as usual—and, after apologizing for running off, pepper them with breathless anecdotes of all the wonderful *animal things* I saw.

It's not the captivity of the animals, strictly speaking, that so disheartens me. I'm sympathetic to their plight, of course, saddened at the extent of their fall. The indolent predators abandoned to denial, which they willingly cultivate through endless hours of sleep. The exasperated primates reduced, in their impotent rage, to hurling hastily assembled fecal projectiles at the jeering schoolboys positioned just out of range. In every cage and tank; every pond and menagerie; ears, tails, wings, fins, tagged with electronic tracking devices and identifying tattoos. It's all very depressing.

I often imagine myself freeing all the animals from their prisons. Why not? It's what we really come to the zoo for, after all. To pretend. Pretend to experience the natural. Pretend to understand and appreciate that which separates us from the animals. Pretend the animals are actually happier under our care, beneath our admiring gaze, than in the dog-eat-dog world from which they were *rescued*.

At first, I liked to pretend that I was one of the animals. A Thompson's gazelle half-hidden in the elephant grass. A surly gorilla stalking a miniature bamboo jungle. A meaty python coiled in reptilian slumber beneath the artificial sun of a heat lamp. I found it easy, at first, to imagine myself in the place of this animal or that. Especially if they had been provided with a suitably simulated environment.

Almost immediately, however, *things* began to press in on my harmless fantasizing. Things like the battered metal door set in the rear wall of the primate habitat which, when open, exposed the veterinary staging area, the concrete floor, the fluorescent ceiling lights, the wire-mesh holding pens *behind* the habitat. Or the electric generator at the edge of the flamingo pond, a thin metal box of flaking green paint, buzzing like a giant mechanical cicada and only partially disguised behind a few scrawny, habitat-specific shrubs. Even the toys in the monkey cage, made from discarded human artifacts, old tires and bleach containers tied to the ends of ropes, were enough to turn everything inside/out. Naturally, the sudden disenchantment effected by these things was compounded by my embarrassment over being forced to apprehend myself in the act of pretending.

My hatred of the zoo, then, is not so much an issue of the animals' lost dignity, as it is a question of habitat.

Pretending to be this animal or that; more importantly, pretending to be this animal or that *in its natural environment.* To be the animal in the murky opacity of its world. That's what I was after. Not pretending to be an animal in a zoo.

This fantasy, my sole source of enjoyment during our repeated trips to the zoo, was so quickly and completely undermined by the untimely and incongruous appearance of base, human objects, that I had already begun to fear going to the zoo, to experience a nervous dread upon arrival. And already, I had begun to test the limits of the parental tether, often turning corners well ahead of them and entering, however briefly, a world beyond their gaze. It's probably no coincidence, then, that my first experience with zoo depression, with my curious, zoo-induced malaise, occurred during the same trip as my first prolonged escape.

I was watching the polar bears. As considerable effort had been made to grace their exhibit with realistic arctic flourishes, I found that by closing my eyes halfway I was able to maintain, to a reasonable degree and despite the midsummer heat, the illusion that I was in fact a lone bear prowling the horizonless polar ice cap. Marshalling all my concentration, I managed to ignore not only the adult bears, lazily sunning themselves atop chiaroscuro mounds of faux ice, but also the two frolicsome cubs, as they barreled across the habitat, attacked each other with playful clumsiness and occasionally tumbled into the large, deep pool of frigid-looking water that formed it's perimeter.

I could not ignore, however, the delight of the spectators thronging about the exhibit. The men in their straw hats and dark glasses, reading loudly and authoritatively from the informational plaque affixed to the railing of the viewing stand, the women fanning themselves with brochures and cooing with cannibalistic maternal envy over the *adorable* cubs and their soft, cuddly *fur*. The irrepressible good humor and carefree contentment of wild animals. Here was the grown-up pretending they had come for.

It was more than I could bear. Grudgingly, I moved on, abandoning my solitary arctic hunt.

Just around the corner, in what amounted to little more than a small cement cubicle with a shallow rectangular pool of water off to one side, its bottom painted powder blue, sat a solitary polar bear, as ancient as he was decrepit. Large patches of bare, irritated flesh stood out pink from his mangy yellow coat. He gave the impression of missing teeth, despite the fact that, as far as I could tell, they were all still accounted for. He sat upright with his back propped against the rear wall of his cell, his hind legs spread-eagled before him. His glaucous eyes fixed, unfocused, on the spot where the concrete floor met the iron bars of his enclosure, he paid little attention to the visitors scuttling quickly past his abode. He was in fact somewhat preoccupied, insofar as he was repeatedly lapping his protracted red penis with slow, methodical licks of his long ruddy tongue. It was unclear how long he had been thus engaged, nor did he show any indication of bringing his activity to a conclusion.

There was an unmistakable air of petulance about this bear, a feeling that, whatever corporeal pleasure might have been derived from the act, the whole thing was actually done out of spite. He was lashing out in the only way left to him, pushing the buttons of the zoo keepers who had clearly given up on him, scandalizing the passing humans doing their utmost to ignore him. This was no longer a bear, this was something like a human, a beast-made-man, a machine programmed to enact a petty cycle of lecherous, self-abasing revenge.

It came to me then, a strange-sounding notion, but undeniably true: not just humans but animals, too, suffer from too much reality, from the menace of shabby things, from elevated levels of transparency, from a poverty of world-sustaining illusion.

That's when the *zoo depression* settled in. It was accompanied by a dehydrated headache, as if I had been crying for hours, by the death of all my future dreams, by the realization that the animal, too, can be made homeless.

home

THERE IS NO SHELTER so mean, no hiding place so farfetched, no refuge so shabby or run down, that it fails to appeal to me as a possible habitation. What's more, this has always been the case.

As a child, no sooner would a cardboard packing box—sent for the holidays by distant relatives, perhaps—be emptied of its contents than I was inside it, demanding just as quickly that the flaps be shut tight behind me.

How at home I was in the tiny space inside. Dark, dry, close, the smaller the better. Once entombed, it took but a minute for flesh and cardboard to establish an equivalent warmth, so that I could no longer distinguish my bare limbs from those parts of the box against which they were pressed, the boundary between self and not-self dissolving into a low-pitched hum of well being. In place of the world, from which I already found myself set apart and at odds, there was only the lively sibilance of my breathing, the hollow, double-time thud of a rabbit's heartbeat reverberating in my ears.

It was as if, inside the box, I was the entire universe.

As if I was everything.

At night, huddled beneath the covers, my face flush in the humid, oxygen-thin atmosphere, my thoughts invariably turned to a singular category of fairy tale character: those diminutive beings fortunate enough, thanks to their fabulous and remarkable dimensions, to have their beds made up in dresser drawers, matchstick boxes, thimbles.

So you'll understand then how it comes to be that not a day goes by without my coming across some mundane refuge or other—an abandoned box, a tarpaulin-covered wood pile, a dilapidated tool shed, a cozy hollow at the base of a tree, a crawlspace—otherwise ordinary enclosures that beckon to me with the allure and terrible insistence of Odysseus' Sirens. I stop in my tracks, close my eyes, feel the drift and sway of my body's every atom in response to the tidal pull of its numinous song.

The strange attraction experienced when confronted by such spaces—standing before the open door of a hushed closet is for me like receiving a summons from some higher power—has been my life's sole constant. It is, quite possibly, the only thing that truly belongs to me. When it comes right down to it, the field of sympathetic oscillations connecting my body to one of these dubious portals *is* me.

None of which makes everyday life any easier.

To walk through a crowded parking lot on a bright summer's day, past the rows of cars shimmering in the late afternoon sun, and think of nothing save the world waiting inside each of their sweltering trunks, close and warm as incubators: it is at once a joy and a torture.

The passage of time is for me a never-ending trial, a continual tug-of-war between the most personal—and therefore the purest—of temptations and the dictates of common sense, of sanity.

For in all other respects I am completely normal. I live in a roomy apartment like everyone else, each day I make my way to and from work, I understand that one simply does not trade in the real world for an empty appliance box or an overturned trash can. Not once have I given in—not since assuming the mantle of adulthood anyway—to the familiar call, to the promise of solipsistic bliss. I have not so much as thrust my head, however briefly, inside a paper bag, not least because I know full well how such a thing would be received.

Still, my deep sense of decorum notwithstanding, there exists another, more important, basis for my restraint: I happen to know that these spaces are not what they seem.

Boxes, trunks, wild animal lairs.

These are not *really* places where one could be at home. Honestly! They are merely *symbols* of the first place, the place that comes before all others. Which is not to say that it's simply a question of some longing for the womb, for a restoration of Eden, for a return to lost origins. These things are impossible, as everyone knows.

It's a question, rather, of an encounter that marks one for life, and in the most fundamental of ways. The source of this encounter need not be a place; it can just as well be a word, a fleeting image, a mundane object, a wandering smell, a person. Usually, the encounter takes place in your earliest days, when you are as yet unaware of the precise coordinates to which every object of experience has already been assigned. Perhaps you were wandering unattended through the house of your grandparents. You turned a corner and there it was, at the end of the hallway: a small ebony clock, its body intricately carved with red, gold and pink roses, a subtly curved crystal protecting and magnifying its meticulously painted face.

Although you have long since forgotten this encounter, you still find yourself unaccountably captivated by a bed of yellow roses, by an elegantly rendered Roman numeral, by the universe that unfolds between the unhurried ticks of an old-world clock.

It has been the secret purpose of my life to to keep the memory of my own encounter alive, to remain faithful to it.

We were traveling by car. An endless day of driving, the destination of which I can no longer recall. I sat alone in the back of our cavernous black sedan, my head resting lazily against the vinyl seat, mesmerized by the rural landscape as it passed by, now blurry, now distinct, by the rhythmic rise and fall of the power cables as they raced from pole to pole.

And then I saw, just off to the side of a wooded border between two farmsteads, a coppice of small firs, planted closely together in a little circle, their tightly interwoven branches forming a low-hanging roof that swayed gently over a bed of dry needles.

In the endless instant before the speeding car bore me away, I was able to imagine an entire life spent inside that tiny wooded realm, an idea of happiness I was to find forever echoed in the derelict enclosures of the real world.

And yet, I never tried to find the circle of little trees. This is due in part to the fact that for some reason I have retained no memory of its precise location. But mostly it's because if I were somehow to stumble upon it again, I would surely discover that they had long since grown tall and sparse and uninviting.

Still, I think every day of my forest, of that space that belongs only to me, of my home.

word made flesh v2.0

And he came to her and said, "Hail, O favored one, The Lord is with you!" But she was greatly troubled at the saying, and considered in her mind what sort of greeting this might be.
- Luke 1:28-29

Angelic Conference Call. From the Office of Chadriel, Junior Vice President for Promotions To Corner of Stanley and Main, Earth.

"Sherman?"

"Yes? This is s/he."

"Chadriel here."

"Yes, I know, what is . . . just a moment . . . Gordriel! Pay attention please! Over *there*? . . . the *bus* and the *stroller*? Yes, handle it, please. Thank you. Sorry Chad. What is it?"

"We need your help."

"Ahhhhhshit."

"*What* did you say?"

"Hosanna. I said 'hosanna.'"

"Quite. Well, anyway, we need you up here for a strategy meeting. ASAP."

"Why me? I'm a little busy, you know? Why don't you get Gabe? S/he is the boss, after all."

"It's *Monday*, Sherman. Gabriel's on the Moon, you know that. Apocalypse run through."

"*Jesus Christ!*"

"Beg your pardon?"

"I said 'cheese and crackers.' Say, have you got me on *speakerphone*?"

"Oh, yeah. Sorry. Tracy and Labriel are here as well."

"Super. You know Chad, there'll be six wars down here if I'm gone for so much as a nano."

"Never mind that. Gabriel will sign off on those."

"That's not the point. Look, what is this about, anyway?"

"It's the Second Coming, Sherman."

"What about it?"

"HE wants it to happen."

"So, what else is new?"

"By the end of the week."

"*Fuuuck*."

"Pardon?"

Avagadro Conference Room, Fibonacci Building, Same Floor. An immeasurably short unit of time later.

His/her left eyebrow cocked meaningfully, Chadriel scanned the shimmering visages of the splendid beings seated around the amber conference table: Sherman, Labriel, Michael, Tracy, Raphael, Uriel. Middle management types, mostly.

"My thanks to you all for coming on such short notice. I've called you here today on a matter of the utmost . . ."

At the far, hierarchically lowest, end of the table, a gaunt, bearded figure, strands of long, greasy hair obscuring much of his face, a *man-form* in other words, raised his thin right arm.

Chadriel sighed pointedly. "Yes, *Judas*. What is it?"

Judas shrugged, coyly innocent. "I don't know, would it be too much to ask to get some hot schwarma or something for one of these meetings? Just once? Vegetarian wraps or *manna* or something? Spring water?"

The room blackened as Michael thundered from across the table, "This is the *spirit* world Judas! There's nothing to eat here!"

Chadriel, his/her full lips pursed, made the palms-out, placating gesture to Michael, then smoothed the front of his/her raiment with his/her flawlessly manicured alabaster hands and turned to Judas. In a calm, pedantic voice, s/he said, "Look, Judas. We've been over this a thousand times, okay? You're a *spirit* now. You've been a spirit for two thousand years, okay? As you may recall, you sort of botched your *task*. You . . ."

Again, the room grew dark. "You were supposed to *surrender yourself* in HIS stead, not turn HIM over, you flea!!"

"Michael, please!"

Grudgingly, Michael restored the lights. Chadriel turned to Judas again, his tone a little less even. "Judas, you're a spirit, it's your *punishment*, okay? This . . . *immateriality* . . . is your prison. Just as it is *ours*. HIS too. I know it's difficult for you, but please try to deal with it, okay?"

A hurt look on his face, Judas collapsed sullenly back into his Aeron chair, its maglev casters gliding a few inches across the polished unobtainium floor.

Sherman muttered under his/her breath, "Double fucking standard."

Michael pounced, ever on the lookout for transgression. "Sorry, what was that, Sherman?"

"I said 'outstanding.'"

Michael shook his head, perplexed. Satisfied with this result, Sherman continued. "It's a double standard, alright? I mean, look at Gabriel. Completely out of touch with what's going on. Armageddon looms, and where is s/he? On the moon, that's where, practicing his/her trumpet. Still floating around in linen and a loincloth of Uphaz gold. *Girded*, s/he calls it. Four thousand year-old golden underwear. I bet s/he hasn't even taken them off since that night in the lion's den."

Chadriel ruffled his/her wings. "That's enough, Sherman."

"I mean, all s/he cares about is moving up the corporate ladder, right? Archangel to *Mercurial* . . ."

"Vice *pres-i-dent*," Chadriel sing-songed.

". . . as if *that* weren't good enough. What does s/he think, they'll actually make him/her *Elohim*? *Seraphim*? Tough job there. Wind the clockwork. Lubricate the celestial mechanics. Sing HIS praises. Bunch of kiss asses." Sherman pointed through the floor, in the direction of Earth. "I'd like to see one of those *higher order* gals last a lunar month down there."

Chadriel's aspect grew terrible.

"Oh, give it a break, Chad. Look, I'm sorry. You know I'm not blaming Gabriel. What else can you expect him/her to expect after the *fall up* from his/her last deal?"

All around the table, winged shoulders sagged, radiant countenances dimmed, silver tongues lolled.

Judas looked around the room. "What? What is it? C'mon, what're you talking about? Do you mean the First Coming?"

Sherman giggled, ignoring Chadriel's warning glance. "Yes, Judas. *The First Coming*."

"*Sher-mun*." Chadriel's tone was cautionary.

"The *Annunciation*. Virgin birth! My God! Look at all the trouble that's caused. Incalculable." Sherman pointed to Judas. "Gabe's as much to blame, or more, as this guy, and for *his/her* punishment they go and make him/her Mercurial?"

Chadriel, exasperated, "We don't say that anymore, Sherman. It's *Vice President* now."

"Oh yes. How could I have forgotten? And how are us mere angels to refer to ourselves again? I've forgotten that too."

"Consultant. Your title is consultant."

"Oh for the love of Pete!"

"It's HIS directive, Sherman."

"Talk about *deal with it*." Sherman spread his/her arms wide. "The whole thing's HIS fault and you know it. A petulant child, that's what HE is."

Michael, unable to temper his/her terrible wrath, leapt from his/her chair onto the table, his/her fiery sword drawn.

Sherman looked up at him/her passively. "Nice touch Mike. Old school. Very Hebrew of you." S/he leaned toward Judas and whispered, "I think *somebody* misses the Hittites."

Judas, still confused as to whether Sherman had actually taken his side, smiled back weakly, while Michael quivered with barely controllable fury.

Ignoring s/him Sherman continued. "It borders on pathetic, this Universe. Let's review: A creation in which the creatures dream of heaven and eternal life—never mind that it's not actually possible for them to attain these things and their true end is to rot in the ground; and the Creator HIMSELF, with but one obsession: to *become* one of those creatures. To draw breath, sleep, rage, hunger, overeat, void HIS bowels, nocturnally *emit*."

Sherman rubbed his/her eyelids in mock fatigue, a gesture s/he had acquired from eons spent among humans, then tucked a lock of golden hair behind his/her ear. "We should have tried harder to talk HIM out of it the last time around, you know? The worst thing is, even though the whole thing was an utter *fiasco*, it still worked well enough for HIM to develop a taste for it."

Chadriel nodded absently. "It would have worked, too, if not for The Traitor, here."

Judas looked around the table for support, shrugging innocently and who-me?-ing.

Sherman shook his/her head. "No, that's not the point, Chad. It should never have gotten that far. But it did, so HE got a big taste and then, just when HE was really starting to have fun, Pilate snatched it away and HE's been pouting ever since, locked away in HIS ROOM. A Creator should have some dignity and abide by the laws of HIS own creation, for Christ's sake. Instead, we're stuck with HIM, sulking since the death of Constantine in the form of that, that ridiculous—" Sherman cast a sideways glance at Chadriel, as if fearing confirmation.

Chadriel sighed forlornly. "Yes, HE still affects the appearance of a giant ceramic statue."

"And is IT still . . .?"

"Renaissance Christ Child? Yes, I'm afraid so."

"That's just wonderful! HE remakes HIMSELF in the anthropomorphic image that we've lead them to believe HE made *them* in to begin with." Sherman massaged his/her temples. "Remember what HE used to call HIMSELF? 'A jealous God'. Talk about self-fulfilling prophecy!"

Michael could no longer contain him/herself. Still atop the table, s/he tensed and shuddered like a ranting professional wrestler, the wildly random oscillations of his/her shimmering form accompanied by a high-pitched whine, steadily increasing in frequency. Smiling sweetly, Sherman brought a hand to his/her pale lips and kissed it, then blew the metaphorical peck toward Michael, who promptly supernovaed.

Chadriel rose painfully from his/her chair, his/her snowy wings fully fanned. "All right. Let's start this over, shall we?"

Cosmic Rewind.

His/her left eyebrow cocked meaningfully, Chadriel scanned the shimmering visages of the splendid beings seated around the amber conference table: Sherman, Labriel, Tracy, Michael, Raphael, Uriel. S/he noted with satisfaction the figure of Judas at the far end of the table, fast asleep.

"My thanks to you all for re-assembling on such short notice. I've called you here today on a matter of the utmost importance. Once again, HE wants a body. There's no talking HIM out of it. More importantly, HE wants it by the end of the week."

Chadriel glanced at Sherman, pausing briefly to allow for objections. None came.

"Right. As you all know, for the bulk of the 5,760 years since the creation of the universe, we have been preoccupied with one overarching problem: HIS desire. Specifically, HIS desire to become human. During this time the Cherubim, Seraphim and other higher order angels have devoted themselves to the non-stop singing of HIS praises, in an effort to raise HIS self-esteem and get HIM to acknowledge HIS *Superior Nature*. So far, it hasn't worked. Nevertheless, they have no plans to suspend their efforts. Thus it has fallen to us, historically, to devise and implement contingencies by which HIS desire may be periodically indulged. Typically, our plans have met with mixed results. This limited success can be attributed primarily to the fact that we have always worked at cross-purposes. It would not be in our best interests—nor HIS, we believe—to lose HIM entirely to this obsession. Thus, we have always sought to maintain a balance between the physical contact HE so desires and HIS fidelity to the role HE created for HIMSELF. Raphael's Olympus Program is still the gold standard here."

Chadriel paused and nodded respectfully to Raphael, who returned a humble smile.

"Not only did the ruse of the Olympic Pantheon provide HIM with frequent intercourse with humans, it also offered a suitable context for HIM to indulge HIS abiding fondness for dress-up." Chadriel sighed nostalgically. "Even the fallout from the Olympus Program was benign, its byproducts settling nicely, upon its inevitable obsolescence, into the pool of world literature, to the lasting benefit of humanity."

For long seconds, total silence—apart from Judas' choppy snoring—fell upon the room, as each of those present reflected fondly on his/her role in the Olympus Program: Nymph, Naïad, Oracle, Satyr.

Shaking him/herself from his/her reverie, Chadriel continued. "Unfortunately, since those *halcyon* days, things have gone steadily downhill. The frequent contact with maidens, heroes and shepherds, far from assuaging HIS desire, only served to intensify it. In response, we devised Operation Chosen People, under the misguided supposition that HE might be satisfied, or at least distracted, if only HE had some humans of HIS very own to care for. We had long taken note of the calming influence of pets on troubled human children. Unfortunately, we failed to notice that the love affair between a child and a tank full of gold fish turns out to be short-lived. So it was with Chosen People. Let's just say *disaster* and speak no more of it.

"In any event, with this monumental blunder we had painted ourselves into a corner. The human psyche, it turns out, possesses no immunity to monotheism. How were we to know that they, in turn, want nothing so much as a shepherd, a big, strong, grandfatherly version of themselves, monitoring their every thought from on high? Never mind that HE was, admittedly, a poor shepherd. HE loathed having to look after them, to speak to them, and as a result decided once and for all that only with a body of HIS own would HE be truly content. The job of securing one was given to Gabriel. The *New Messianic Plan*. Miracles, parables, holy mothers, hookers, devilish temptation—nice work there, Sherman— Romans, brotherly love." Chadriel stared across the room at the slumbering form of Judas, his head now resting on the table, a thin stream of saliva silvering from the corner of his open mouth and pooling on the amber tabletop. "And let's not forget Gethsemane."

Chadriel drew a deep breath. "Well, it's Go time once again, and we need a plan. I've already spoken with Gabriel. S/he favors annunciation, for what I consider to be less than objective reasons. Be that as it may, s/he's currently a little preoccupied with end-of-days stuff, and has left the design and implementation of a suitable plan entirely to our discretion. Let me be clear: I am against another annunciation. First of all, there are its inherent limitations; specifically, the fact that the suggestion, the message, must be delivered to a suitably impressionable young woman—one who is unaware, who does not even suspect, that she is pregnant—in order for HIM to successfully commandeer the fetus. Second, the scope of such an announcement is rather limited, seeing as how it can only, by definition, be broadcast to an audience of one. Finally, I'd like to pull this one off without exacerbating the religion thing. In fact, if at all possible, I'd like to bypass religion altogether. It's a Chinese finger trap really, and we've foisted it on them for the purpose of accommodating our own designs for far too long. I'd really rather we stop lying to them and let them get on with the job of living and dying," s/he glanced at Sherman, "and *decaying* in peace. Are there any objections—any *serious* objections—at this point?"

Silence. Snoring.

"Good. Well, then. Let's start from the top. What're our options for doing this thing according to more solid *scientific* principles? Uriel?"

Uriel, who had been absorbed for some time in the effort to pat his/her head at the same time as s/he rubbed his/her stomach in an alternating clockwise/counterclockwise motion, looked up suddenly, then cleared his/her throat. "0001 0110 1010 0010 1101 0100 . . ."

"Uriel."

Uriel stopped and looked at Chadriel, a blank expression on his/her face.

"In *Anglish*, please."

"Ah, yes. Of course. Well, we've two major projects in the works. First off, we have for some time now been employing what you might call an evolutionary fast track, by means of which we hope to instantiate a God-center within the human brain. This God-center would, theoretically, make any and all human bodies accessible to HIM."

"And what is the status of this project?"

"Well, up until the mid 19TH century, it was coming along nicely. We had—all within the space of two millennia, mind you—managed to raise a small nodule in the left temporal lobe. When fully developed, this nodule—or Godule, as we jokingly referred to it in the lab—would have acted as a kind of literal-reality cockpit, from which HE would be able to enjoy, real time, the unmediated experience of any human organism—or all of them at once, for that matter. Emotions, sensations, what have you. At the same time, we had identified a suitable 'prophet.' Franz Joseph Gall, a committed materialist, the father of phrenology. The development of his *intuitive* science was to be the lynchpin of our efforts to eradicate the memetic persistence of body/soul dualism once and for all. Despite the fact that the Godule was not yet complete, Gall was already zeroing in on it, having surrounded its actual location, in his phrenological topography, with metaphorical organs for spirituality, veneration, benevolence, sublimity, theosophy and the like."

Chadriel straightened in his/her seat, erect with hope. "And?"

Uriel had once again lapsed into a blank stare. "Hmm? Oh, yes. Well, like all materialists, Gall ended up persecuted and ridiculed, a broken man. All in HIS name, ironically enough. His work was discredited, materialism was buried beneath an avalanche of positivist hubris and neo-dualist empiricism from which it has yet to fully re-emerge, and development of the Godule came to a standstill."

Michael huffed, indignant. "And that's it? Two thousand years of high priced R&D, all for naught?"

"Well, not entirely. We set aside a couple of interns to continue working on the Godule, a move which turned out, if I may say so myself, to be quite prescient."

"Oh really? And why is that?"

"Well, the Godule has, quite recently, been rediscovered."

"You don't say?"

"Yes. A group of neuroscientists in New Brunswick have established contact with the Godule by means of transcranial magnetic stimulation."

Chadriel's brow furrowed, betraying his/her distaste of locutions that smacked of scientific arcana. "Which *is*?"

"A religion helmet."

Sherman snorted.

Uriel continued. "Well, that's what they're calling it. It's not really a helmet. Actually, it's nothing more than a carefully modulated electrical current, applied to a highly localized portion of the left temporal lobe, i.e. the Godule."

"And what is it, exactly, that the *religion helmet* does?"

"Well, it induces in the test subject ecstatic, mystical visions of the Godhead."

Chadriel collapsed onto the table, his/her head buried in his/her arms. At length, s/he looked up and, in response to Uriel's uncomprehending stare, said, "Well that's not exactly going to do the trick, is it?"

Uriel still didn't get it. Sherman cut in, "Look, Uri, what were trying to do here is get HIM control of a human body, not give *them* a means of communicating with HIM. I mean, there wouldn't be much point of shipping HIM off to this Godule of yours just so HE could get stuck in some recursive loop of visions of HIMSELF, now, would there?"

Uriel nodded in agreement. "Nope. That would be pointless."

Michael began to quake, ever so slightly.

Chadriel waved his hands about testily, as if to clear the air in front of him/her of noxious vapors. "Okay, okay. Never mind that. You mentioned two projects. What is the second?"

"Hmmm? Oh. Well, we've been exploring the feasibility of fabricating a body—it's more like a suit, really—out of elementary particles."

"And? Is it?"

"Hmmm?"

"*Feasible*? Is it feasible?"

"Oh yes. Very much so. Currently, sixty percent of our neutrino suits maintain field integrity for as long as six weeks."

"And the other forty percent? What happens to them?"

"We're not exactly sure. They don't maintain field integrity, I can tell you that. We think it's a problem with the, ah, *connective tissue*, if you will. We're out of quintessence—we put an order in ages ago, you may recall—and so we've had to make do with gluons, which as you know are not nearly as reliable. We do have a suit that utilizes prototype ubergluons, which seems to have solved the problem, whatever it was."

Tentatively, Raphael raised his/her hand. Sherman shook his/her head in disbelief as Chadriel gestured impatiently. "Yes, Raphael. Go ahead."

"How does this suit compare to a real human body?"

"Oh, well it's far superior, of course."

"No, no. What I mean is, will it *feel* like a human body, to HIM?"

"Oh yes. The whole thing's run by a state of the art neural net. Flawless reproductions of the human perceptual system. HE wouldn't even have to go to earth, really. We could run the whole thing in HIS ROOM, if we wanted."

Chadriel nodded impatiently. "Yes, of course. But assuming we *want* to send HIM to earth, what are the risks?"

Uriel thought for a moment. "Well, to be honest, we haven't exactly focused on a delivery system. As it stands right now, I'd say there's a ninety-plus percent chance the neutrino suit would shoot him straight through one side of the earth's crust and out the other. That's assuming HE doesn't get trapped a mile underground in some 40-ft-diameter acrylic particle-detecting vessel filled with 7,000 tons of deuterium. Statistically highly unlikely, of course, but possible."

It was Chadriel's turn to massage his/her temples. "Uriel. How long will it take to have a structurally reliable suit ready, with a foolproof delivery system?"

Uriel hesitated for a moment, calculating. Then, "Eighteen months."

Sherman chuckled. Uriel shrugged. Darkness.

"NOT EXACTLY A *WEEK*, IS IT?!" Michael shouted.

Chadriel threw his/her hands up in exasperation. "Look, forget it. We don't have time for this. We need a plan, and we have a week—minus Sunday—to get it done, all right? At this point, I'm open to anything."

His/her dark eyes full of apparent sadness, Tracy said, "There's no other way, Chadriel. It'll have to be annunciation."

Looking for help, Chadriel turned to Sherman, who simply shrugged his/her shoulders, as if to say, *Afraid so.*

Softly, Chadriel pounded his/her forehead. "Okay then. So be it. But please, let's at least try to make some improvements this time. For starters, I'd like to avoid having one of us appearing in our true form. And maybe this time we can make it clear from the get-go who and *what* HE really is so the authorities don't end up sending HIM to the gas chamber, or the chair, or whatever they use these days. Sherman, I'm open to suggestions here."

Sherman reclined his/her Aeron chair as far as it would go. At length, s/he said, "You know, the statue thing suggests an interesting possibility. I mean, even as we speak, there are people flocking to a backyard in Milwaukee, just to see an image of Jesus in an otherwise random collection of knots at the base of a tree. Never mind the fact that if the half-dead tree is gestalting anything, it's an anthropomorphic Sunday school image. My point is, the human brain is wired to see faces in almost anything. Electrical outlets, oil slicks, plates of food. All it takes is three dots, really. Given that, and the fact that they're always on the lookout for miracles, maybe the announcement could be made by a giant statue in some city center. I think they could accept that. Plus, there's bound to be any number of undetected pregnancies in a big city crowd."

Chadriel nodded appreciatively. "I like it. Let's tone the statue angle down a bit though. I'd like to keep the medium along slightly more secular lines, okay? And let's keep it one-on-one for the time being. Good. Excellent. Yes. Well, let's make it happen."

The others began to shimmer and dissolve . . .

"Oh, and one last thing, just so you're aware of what's at stake. If this doesn't work out, HE'S tearing it all apart—us included—and starting over. In a week's time, Gabriel could very well be blowing that trumpet of his/hers. I, for one, would prefer if that didn't happen, okay?"

7:05 A.M. *Corrigan Residence, Dundas, Ontario, Canada.*

COAST deodorant soap is best known, and rightfully so, for its zingy, eye-opening freshness. Sean Corrigan, however, prized the blue-green cleansing cake not for its uncanny ability to jumpstart his day, but, rather, for its consistency. When wet, it turns out, a COAST bar's soft, buttery surface provides the ideal medium for the inscription of love notes. Such was the highlight of Sean's morning shower, always taken while his wife was still fast asleep: inscribing in the soap, usually with his thumbnail, little reminders of his love. He would then return the soap to its tray, where the message would silently await her late-morning arrival. Nothing elaborate or ostentatious, mind you. A simple I ♥ U, for example. Or a ☺. Or a pet name. Or, occasionally, something a little more risqué. Whether or not she actually read, or even noticed these soapy missives, was another matter. Either way, Sean had been diligently writing them since before they we married.

Today, however, was going to be a little different. He could hardly believe it himself. After six years of marriage, he had finally convinced Claire that they were ready to bring another life into their happy household. Or at least to start trying.

Today, he thought as he guided the bar over broad forearms and shoulders, over stocky thighs and calves, beneath armpits and behind knees, *today will mark the beginning of a new trend. From now on*, he thought proudly, *I'll come up with a prospective name each day, write it on the soap. Then later, at supper maybe, I'll see what she thinks.* Sean whistled—Onward Christian Soldiers!—as he stabbed at the sections of his lower back that were still within reach, then slid the sudsy bar into the abyssal divide between his hairy buttocks before moving, finally, to his testicles, which he treated to a vigorous but entirely wholesome once-over.

Where to start? he thought. Well, that was easy enough. Sean had always been partial to biblical names. *Old testament or New? Might as well start at the beginning,* he thought. He ran down the list alphabetically (for some reason he could only come up with male names): *Aaron, Abraham, Caleb, Daniel, Ezekiel, Isaac, Jacob, Jeremiah, Jonah, Joshua* ... Joshua. *Now there's a good one!* he thought. An image of the young John Derek flashed across his consciousness. *Nice diminutive too. Josh. Well, it's a start, anyway. Get the ball rolling.* Sean set the bar down, then quickly washed and rinsed his hair and turned off the water. He picked the soap up once again and was about to write his suggestion on it when he noticed that a number of short, wiry red hairs were stuck to it. Hardly the message he wanted to convey. Despite the fact that the hairs were his, Sean winced with a kind of embarrassed disgust. *Well, that won't do, will it?* He raised a forefinger to the bar, then stopped to look at the arrangement of hairs more closely. He chuckled softly to himself. It looked just like the incomparable Gretzky. Oiler team photo, 1985. Sean's thoughts turned to memories of greatness: Gretzky, Messier, Kurri, Fuhr. Then he remembered why he was holding the bar in the first place: *Josh.* Hurriedly, he scraped the hairs off with his nail, before the face they had formed had a chance to speak to him.

~

8:20 A.M. *Silva Residence, 37 Jericho Road, Garden Home West Mobile Home Park, Binghamton, New York, USA.*

Amid the frightful chaos that engulfed the kitchenette, a fury of sound and motion, Danilo Silva sat inert, a veritable Gibraltar. Danilo handled breakfast in the Silva household. Not that there was much to it. Pour bowls of breakfast cereal, administer sober portions of Hi-C, arbitrate the disputes that inevitably arose over proximity and chewing sounds, pack the school lunches. Even so, it was all he could do to manage it. This morning, for example: three bowls of Lucky Charms, one Apple Jacks, one Crunch Berries, another a medley of all three combined; six shot glasses of grape juice. All that and fifteen year-old Danny Jr. hadn't even made his appearance yet. Danilo thought about going in and rousing the boy, then decided against it. Something in Rose's eye told him Jr. didn't come home last night. Oblivious to the jostling and shouting all around him, Danilo stared at the tabletop. Only thirty-three, and already he lived in fear of becoming a grandfather. And Encarnacíon, only thirty-one.

In a way, having kids was all Danilo had ever known. Danny Jr. was a high school accident, of course. Rose, too, now that he thought about it. At the moment there were seven of them. It was the only thought in his mind, as he sat there: *I've got to do it before it happens again.* And therein lay the problem. How to get the money, the day off work, have the surgery, recover, all without Encarnacíon ever knowing. And all before it happened again. He sat there without blinking, his coffee lukewarm and untouched.

Rose, just turned fourteen, stepped nicely into the power vacuum left by Jr's absence. She, at least, noticed that there was something wrong with dad. Danilo smiled weakly to himself. What a kid. She would handle it. Realizing that it was time to leave for school, she rousted the others from the table, admonishing them to bus their own dishes. It almost worked. Of the six bowls, four actually made it to the sink. The other two clattered, in concert, to the floor; that would be the twins, Scott and Todd. Danilo looked over at the spill, then up at Rose, already with a towel in her hand.

"It's okay," he said. "Just leave it. I'll take care of it."

He smiled weakly again, then went back to staring at the table. Rose threw the towel into the sink, doled out the brown paper bags, buttoned up coats, strapped on backpacks. Then, without a word, she led her brothers out the door.

Wearily, Danilo pushed himself from the table and went to the sink for a sponge. He stepped absently to the spill, then dropped to his knees to clean it. He jerked upright, drawing his breath in sharply. There, spread out before him on a canvas of buckled linoleum and spilt milk, was a face, rendered in Crunch Berries and Apple Jacks. By squinting a little, Danilo was able to throw the image into sharper relief. It was not just any face. He could hardly believe his eyes. There was no denying it. It was like a miracle. Right there on his kitchenette floor. The face of Kurt Cobain.

His mind raced. It had to be some kind of sign, a good omen maybe. What to do? Above all, he wanted to show someone. He thought about waking Encarnacíon, then shook his head. *She won't see it. Or worse, she'll see the Pope or the Virgin or something.* No, it would be better if she didn't see it at all. He turned from the apparition, looking over his shoulder toward the bedroom, just as Encarnacíon stepped into the bathroom and closed the door behind her. Danilo heard a clink as the toilet seat was lifted, then a muffled coughing that sounded a little like retching.

Well. That's that.

His day nearly salvaged by the strange event, Danilo Silva sighed, fell back upon his hands and knees and began sponging up the spill.

3:05 P.M. *BP Filling Station & Convenience Mart, Corner of Young and Palmyra, Provo, Utah, USA.*

Amy Smith turned the wobbly analog dial, setting the microwave timer to two minutes. The instructions on the back of the Bagel Dog wrapper said to heat it on one side for a minute and a half, then turn it over for another minute and a half, then remove it from the oven and let it cool for one minute. But she was *sooo* hungry, there was no way in heck she was going to wait a full four minutes. Lukewarm would be good enough.

Amy ran the tips of her fingers across the front of her wool sweater, sounding for snags. She found one on the nail of her index finger and promptly brought it to her mouth, gnawing at it feverishly. She was *sooo* stressed lately. And so hungry all the time. She tried not to think about it, but knew she must have put on ten pounds in the last month. *What in Pete's name is wrong with me?* Tears welled up in her eyes. *Why can't I stop eating?*

The microwave reached the T-minus-one-minute mark. Already, the air around the microwave was filled with the savory aroma of expanding hot dog meat. Amy felt the telltale tug in her stomach, her mouth filling up with saliva a split-second later. For the moment, she pushed her worries aside. She would probably finish it off in three bites. Then, if she had enough money, she would probably buy another one. Still gnawing on her finger, she reached into her purse with her other hand, groping absently for her wallet. She felt a mild panic. *Where's my wallet?* Setting her purse on the counter next to the microwave, she rifled through it hurriedly. Her wallet was not there.

Maybe it's in the car. It must be in the car. Please, Lord, tell me I didn't leave it at work.

Thirty-five seconds and counting. She slung her purse over her shoulder and scurried through the doors, past the disapproving eyes of the cashier and out to her car. Her heart sank as a quick search of her car turned up nothing. Again, her eyes filled with tears. Then she pulled out the ashtray. Forty-five cents. What was the Bagel Dog? $1.95. She looked down. Pennies, nickels, dimes, scattered all over the floor of the car. There was hope. Still fighting back tears, she began scraping together the necessary change.

Inside the store, the Bagel Dog kept cooking. The timer, as happened every so often, was stuck on thirty seconds.

From behind the counter, Gambriz Tablisi watched the stupid white woman climb into the driver's seat of her car and close the door. She sat there for a moment. Then Gambriz could see her body begin to shake. *Was the stupid lady crying? What for?* Gambriz laughed aloud as she began pounding the steering wheel with her fists. *Have a nice day, stupid lady!* he thought as she pulled away from her parking space and screeched off into the traffic.

Thhuuunnkk!!!

Gambriz tore his admiring gaze from the gleaming new Ford Extrusion rumbling into the lot and glanced over at the food preparation center. Something had exploded in the microwave again. *Stupid piece of crap!* Reluctantly, Gambriz grabbed a roll of paper towels went over to the stupid oven.

He opened the door, then recoiled in disgust. Stupid pig meat, splattered all over the inside. *Stupid fucking white lady!* Gambriz launched into a torrent of obscenities as he unraveled a wad of paper towels from the roll, bracing himself for the task at hand. Since he couldn't bring himself to look at the *disgusting filth* as he wiped it up, he couldn't possibly have registered the uncanny similarity the configuration of splattered meat bore to his own state senator, Orrin Hatch. Nor, given the strident vehemence of his ranting, could he have been expected to hear the soulless recitation of its pre-recorded utterance: *Hail, O favored one* . . .

Chadriel's Office.

Sherman regarded Chadriel's aura sympathetically. "You look like death warmed over, Chad."

Chadriel sighed. "Never mind that." S/he looked up at Sherman, his/her eyes narrowing. "I'm sure these annunciation attempts you've orchestrated so far are not really as pathetic as they seem. Pure bad luck, unforeseeable contingencies, that sort of thing. Right? This is no joke, Sherman; you understand the consequences of failure as well as anyone. I'd like to believe there's no reason to doubt that you and your crew are giving this your full attention." Chadriel furrowed his/her brow. "It's hardly the time for sandbagging."

Changing the subject, s/he said, "You know Sherman, you've done a wonderful job with the whole Lucifer bit."

Sherman shot a warning glance at Chadriel. "Let's not get into that again, shall we?"

"It was always meant to be a short-term thing, Sherman, a temporary theological nicety. There was no choice, really. HE needed a scapegoat."

Sherman smiled sweetly. "Everybody needs a scapegoat, Chad."

"Well, all I'm trying to say is, you did your part, it's appreciated, it really is. But maybe you're stuck in your role, hmm? Anyway, I'm taking you off two-point-oh. We can't risk any more failures. The consequences are simply too great."

"*And?*"

"And, I don't trust you, Sherman. I'm sorry, I just can't shake the feeling that you're trying to pull this all down."

"How long have we been at this, Chad? You know as well as I that things are more then capable of coming down on their own. It's the underlying principle of this whole fucking *creation*, in my *humble* opinion."

Chadriel stared hard at Sherman.

Sherman shook his/her head, still smiling. "Okay, fine. So what are *your* plans, if I might ask?"

Chadriel sat up, suddenly enthusiastic. "Well, something on a slightly larger scale, for starters. I'm thinking glass skyscraper, somewhere on the Pacific Rim. No more of this *North America*. I'm through dealing with Christians. Tokyo, Shanghai, Kuala Lumpur. Lunch hour, thousands of people milling about, and then, boom! the message, thirty stories tall and plain as day, right on the side of the building. No missing it. I can already see it."

"And what will the message say, exactly?"

"Well, I don't know yet. Something unambiguous, I can tell you that much."

Sherman leaned back in his/her chair, picturing the scene. Thousands of preoccupied humans darting about, lost in their own fears, desires, appetites. Looking straight-ahead, unseeing. Looking down at the ground, unseeing. Sneaking peeks at each other's flesh. Even so, a few of them would undoubtedly look up and take note of Chadriel's message. *That will have to be dealt with.* A thin smile crossed his/her lips at the thought. Yes, s/he could see *that*, too. A giant, automated window cleaner, slowly, methodically, working its way down the building's glass and aluminum façade, just in time to squeegee the annunciation of the second coming from view.

the thereminist

A YEAR AGO my friend Todd—he's a friend of a friend, really—announced that he'd just bought a second-hand theremin and a small, battery powered amplifier, with the apparent intention of performing for money in the local subway stations. I distinctly remember the irritation with which I greeted this announcement, dismissing it instantly as simply the latest in an endless series of his heavy-handed attempts to draw attention to himself. It was essentially a childish stunt (and

Todd was nothing if not childish), one which could only have meaning for him and his immediate circle of friends, the type of thing the rest of us had long since foregone. There would be a brief outbreak of excitement and interest: *You HAVE to go check out Todd tomorrow in Central station, it's ABSOLUTELY hilarious.* And then, just as quickly, the whole thing would grow stale and disappear from our loose network's collective discourse, memorialized only by the one or two actually funny anecdotes that the two-week period of tedious pretension was sure to generate. Worse still, I had no doubt that, despite it's money-making pretensions, Todd's new calling would not signal an end to his penchant for hitting us up for loans and handouts.

There was no reason to expect his new *enterprise* to do anything other than fail utterly. To begin with, there's the fact that he was completely without musical training. Which is not to say that even a trained musician could coax anything from a theremin worth paying for. But with his skill level, it was not an over-reaction to fear that Todd was putting himself at risk of violent physical attack. Second, there was the simple fact that everything he did tended to end in minor catastrophe.

So I must admit to my surprise upon being told, just yesterday, that he was still at it. What's more, if what people are saying is correct, he's actually making a pretty fat living off of it, often taking in well over a hundred dollars for just a couple hours' work. Indeed, if the rumors are to be believed, he is apparently now something of a fixture on the city's subway platforms.

I was puzzled, to say the least. Had he somehow gained actual mastery over the bizarre instrument, figured out some means of duping it into yielding strains and melodies that human ears actually found tolerable, perhaps even enjoyable?

As it turns out, he had done nothing of the sort, and is presently no more able to play a chord on command than he had been at the start. No. He makes his money, it seems, not by playing his theremin, but by *not* playing it. This is how my informant explained Todd's technique to me, related to her, she said, by Todd himself:

The very first morning, he walked to the station nearest his apartment and positioned himself on the platform near the bottom of the escalator. He set his theremin up on its microphone stand, jacked it into the amplifier, and set about calibrating the instrument; or rather, calibrating the position of his body in relation to it. Intrigued as much by the novelty that the theremin is played without being touched as by the science-fictionesque chirps and strangely pleasing low-end moans burping from his amp, a few heads from the crowd of morning commuters turned in his direction. He stood before the small, black, rectangular console for long seconds, perfectly still. Then he let loose with a torrent of soul-splitting noise, an offensive, unholy clamor fully protected by his First Amendment rights. The amp shrieked and bellowed like a mad whale. The hapless commuters, stranded between incoming trains, put as much distance between themselves and Todd as they could manage, but it was futile, the demonic din reverberated off the curved walls, filling every square inch of the subterranean vault. There was no escape.

Then, just when he had pushed his victims to the brink of a mobbish frenzy, Todd pulled out a pair of headphones and plugged them into a jack on the theremin's front panel.

The aural onslaught ceased.

The noise filling the station gradually dissipated, echoing faintly as it escaped down the tunnels to either side. No sooner had silence returned in full than the first bill had fallen in Todd's cardboard collection box.

It was extortion, basically.

I had to hand it to him. I would have never given him credit for coming up with such a reliable, time-honored means of making a living. By the end of his first week, he was able to dispense with the preliminary cacophony altogether. Now, apparently, he spends no more than a couple hours a day in one station or another.

And for those couple of hours he stands there—headphones on, stock still except for his hands, which dance artfully about the instrument—prepared to visit his righteous fury upon the heads of the city's professionals should the money cease to flow into his ever-growing box.

2050 or, what it was like

Today the modernist spirit prophesies its own glorious annihilation, followed by a state of ultimate lucidity, when it will continue to dominate the relics of the material world.
- Raoul Vaneigem

Narrowing his uncommonly close-set eyes in the semi-darkness, the President stared at the images before him, pondering. The scientists—futurologists, in fact—watched him anxiously, unsure perhaps of his immediate reaction to their admittedly alarming presentation. The military men, for their part, were not overly concerned. The President was a plodder. Given enough time he would connect the dots for himself. Once he did, they knew, there would be nothing to worry about. His response would be entirely appropriate.

Still squinting, the President plied the cleft of his clean-shaven chin with his thumb, seemingly lost in thought. The exact words the scientists had used, their precise implications, had already receded beyond recall, sucked out to the murky beyond of his short term memory like the waning Bay of Fundy tidewaters to the Atlantic abyssal. Fortunately the pictures were still there, glowing impressively—*Like magic*, the President thought—on the giant rectangle of thick Lucite that rose from the center of the 20-seat oval conference table.

The President looked again at the luminous earth mapped out on the left side of the panel, white land masses set against a royal blue oceanic background, the various nations delineated in light gray. Large portions of the map, land and sea, were overlaid with oval- and kidney-shaped blobs of color. He was reminded, happily, of those central-command maps once used to track the numerous theatres of a world war, the kind with the colored-flag push pins and the miniature naval fleets and armored divisions. For the time being, he avoided looking at the bulleted lists on the center and right sections of the panel, labeled "Global Warming Timeline" and "Likely Outcomes," respectively.

Instead, he shifted his gaze to the color-coded legend at the bottom of the map. He looked at the first colored square, *Tan*, then read the caption: *Deforestation*. His eyes traveled automatically to the distinctive outline of the American mainland. No tan. He noted with satisfaction that Canada and most of Mexico were also *tan free*. His face already considerably more relaxed, the President scanned the remaining nations. All the countries sandwiched between the bottom of Mexico and the top of South America were completely filled in with tan, as were the Philippines, Malaysia (or Indonesia, he wasn't sure which), significant swaths of central Africa and southeast Asia, and the top part of Russia. *The former Soviet Union.* The President's countenance grew stern at the thought.

Methodically, he went through the list of colored squares, reading the caption next to each one and identifying its corresponding theatre of calamity on the map:

> *Aquamarine. Increased severity/frequency of tropical storms:* The Pacific's Asian rim; the Indian coast; the Caribbean islands (Cuba!); Florida.
>
> *Pale blue. Primary fisheries affected:* Iceland; Britain; Scandinavia; Japan.
>
> *Green. Decreasing crop yield:* Africa.
>
> *Blue-gray. Rising sea level:* Mediterranean Europe; North Africa; India; Australia; Florida.
>
> *Pink. Increased disease risk:* Europe; Central Africa; Southeast Asia; Russia; the Eastern seaboard.
>
> *Gray. Water conflicts: . . . ?*

The President made a couple of passes over the map, but was unable to locate the supposed water conflicts. *Maybe they haven't figured out where those go yet.*

"What's that green and gray striped color mean?" he asked. "I don't see a square for that."

The scientists exchanged glances. One of them, the goateed one, replied, "The green and gray stripes represent areas affected by significant loss of crops *in addition* to conflicts over water, Mr. President."

The President looked back at the map. South America, Africa, Asia. He nodded astutely. Wagging a forefinger at the display, he asked, "What about seismic activity?"

This time the bearded scientist deferred the question to his bald colleague, who had pushed his glasses up onto his forehead and was rubbing his eyes wearily. "At this point, Mr. President, we're not really able to correlate the relationship between global warming and seismic activity."

The President regarded him thoughtfully. "I see." Clasping his hands behind his head, he leaned back in his chair, the first faint signs of a smile crossing his face. If what the blobs of color said was true, things could have been *a heck of a lot worse*. Indeed, the President had already identified, *for his money*, the most important graphic, the nearly unsullied white of the North American continent.

Reminding himself that there was more, he took a deep breath, bracing himself for the effort. From his reclined position, his feet now resting on the tabletop, he forced himself to peruse the "Global Warming Timeline":

> *2007: Violent storms smash coastal barriers rendering large parts of the Netherlands uninhabitable. Cities like The Hague are abandoned. In California the delta island levees in the Sacramento river area are breached, disrupting the aqueduct system transporting water from north to south.*
>
> *2010: The US and Europe will experience a third more days with peak temperatures above $90^{\circ}F$.*
>
> *2010 – 2020: Siberian weather patterns envelope Britain and Europe (annual temperature drop of $6^{\circ}F$).*

Alright, that's enough! he said to himself. This was the kind of thing that always got his goat. Was he really supposed to believe that, starting in 2010, the temperature in Europe was going to go up *and* down at the same time? He made a mental note to have the scientists to pick one or the other. He wasn't about to come out looking the fool on account of *their* indecisiveness.

His concentration broken, the President spot-read the rest of the time line. More dire predictions about the weather, more things that sounded to him like contradictions. Irritated, he skipped to the end to see how far this whole time line went. 2050.

Unimpressed, he turned his attention to the right side of the panel, where the "Likely Outcomes" were listed in forest green, his favorite color. It was a long list, too long by his standards, but even so it held his interest. His reclining figure growing ever more erect, the President read, enthralled:

> *Climate becomes an 'economic nuisance.'*
>
> *Access to water becomes a major battleground.*
>
> *A 'significant drop' in the planet's ability to sustain its present population becomes apparent over the next 20 years.*
>
> *Deaths from war and famine run into the hundreds of millions until the planet's population is reduced by such an extent the Earth can cope.*
>
> *Mega-droughts affect the world's major breadbaskets, including the Midwest, where strong winds bring soil loss. People stop eating bread.*
>
> *China's huge population and food demand make it particularly vulnerable, resulting in the revocation of Most Favored Nation*

trading status. After the consumption of all crops, animals and insects, the Chinese resort to eating each other. The remnants of Chinese "society" reorganize around the economic and cultural realities of anthropophagia.

Bangladesh becomes nearly uninhabitable due to rising sea level, which contaminates the inland water supplies. Nevertheless, millions continue to inhabit it, living in floating cities made from abandoned cargo ships, inflatable rafts and flotsam.

Riots and internal conflict tear apart India, South Africa and Indonesia. Following the rapid exhaustion of tactical nuclear arsenals, wars are fought hand-to-hand, with machetes, farm implements and poison blow darts.

The deforested Balkans are overrun by packs of wild dogs and lycanthropes, which terrorize the Catholic and Eastern Orthodox Christian populations. Blood hungry Vampyri reclaim ancestral estates in Romania and northern Hungary.

Europe faces huge internal struggles as it copes with massive numbers of migrants washing up on its shores. The establishment of bio-chemical "forbidden zones" around the borders of G7 (renamed to accommodate Russia's return to feudalism) member states brings some relief.

Rich areas like the US and Europe become 'virtual fortresses.' Subjected to occasional disruptions in satellite telephone service, periodic soft drink shortages, and long lines at surgical enhancement centers, the citizens of these countries turn to the evangelically-controlled entertainment industry for solace.

The President's pulse quickened as he read through the list. At last, a black-and-white world picture was being sketched for him, an apocalyptic world in which all the troublesome gray confusions were gone. A world precariously and deliciously balanced on the edge of disaster. A world requiring strong leadership. Steadfastness. Resolve. It was a thrilling prospect. He felt a sense of exhilaration rising in his chest. His perineum tingled.

A random montage, culled from twentieth century disaster films and death camp news reels, from millenarian bible comics and Save the Children infomercials, began piecing itself together in his head. He was now sitting bolt upright in his chair, transfixed by the images parading past his mind's eye: gargantuan tsunamis erasing the fundamentalist, economically competitive nations of the Pacific archipelagoes; legions of swarthy, famine-stricken eastern Europeans crushed up against the border fences of their civilized neighbors; Africa consumed by the Sahara, the entire continent an endless sea of starving, distended bodies, flies swarming about inert, expressionless eyes; *Mr. President?*; Moscow abandoned, interred for an age beneath the burgeoning permafrost; Britain restored to the Celtic tribes; *Sir?*; Ohio-class submarines and genetically-enhanced flipper men patrolling the waters along the Philadelphia coast; a neo-New Deal, millions of Americans unemployed once again and swelling the ranks of a bottomless labor army, eternally engaged in the construction and fortification of The Great Border Wall. *Mr. President?*

He opened his eyes. Across the table, the pointy-bearded scientist was regarding him intently. "Sir? Is everything alright?" The President cast a quick glance at Rear Admiral Stuckey. The Admiral, his moist eyes sparkling in the diodic light, nodded knowingly. *Yes. It's all true.*

The President had to suppress a laugh. He turned to the scientist, brusquely dismissing his concern. "Fine. I'm fine. Look, you're absolutely convinced that these things are gonna happen?"

Again, the scientists exchanged glances. "Yes sir. Assuming 'business as usual' the likelihood of their occurrence is quite high."

The President looked around the table smugly, oblivious to the thinly veiled sarcasm of the bearded scientist's remark. "Business As Usual" was his personal motto. With a mental smirk, he recalled how horrified his advisors had been when he informed them of his decision to adopt it as his campaign slogan. The smirk bloomed into a smile. It certainly hadn't kept him from getting re-elected. His gut instinct had been right. *As usual.* And now this report. Finally, it seemed, his steadfastness, his resolve, his commitment to *Business As Usual* was going to start paying some dividends.

Then, from out of nowhere, a lone dark cloud appeared, creeping inexorably across the vast, uninterrupted plain of the President's psyche before settling directly overhead, its irksome shadow obscuring the world-to-come CGI blockbuster screening in his head. This storm cloud, this ominous, solitary stain, was actually just a thought. A number, in fact: 2050.

The President's expression clouded. Reluctantly, he did the math. 2050 *minus* 2004. That was something like 50 years. Slipping his hands beneath the table, he subtracted the years on his fingertips, eventually arriving at the remainder, 46. Applying the same mechanism, he added forty-six years to his current age.

He gasped.

104*!*

The image of that number planted itself in his field of vision like a giant boulder before the gates of heaven, a sinister, immovable object barring his passage to paradise.

His brow furrowed. *In 2050, I'll be 104 years old. I might be dead by then.*

Placing his hands squarely on the table in front of him, the President breathed deeply, his head shaking slightly as his eyes darted about the room in search of a reassuring face.

It was the turn of the scientists—futurologists, in fact—to smile. Maybe their report would have the desired effect after all. Their only goal, coming into this initial meeting, had been to resolve one simple point for the President. *Something must change.* Either the policies of the industrialized nations would have to be drastically altered, and soon, or the very tenor of human life on the planet would be in serious jeopardy.

The military men, of course, read the President's agitation—the flush rapidly spreading across his neck, the beads of sweat accumulating on his upper lip, the soft fluttering of his right eyelid—somewhat differently. *He has the facts now. He'll understand. His response to this crisis will be entirely appropriate.*

Already, they could see, he had come to a decision.

The President's hands rose from the table even before he began to speak. As if driven by a mind of their own, they automatically formed the empty gestures that he had long ago been told must accompany his every official utterance. He cleared his throat.

"Jennelmen, the task before us is clear. Let there be no doubt. It is a difficult task. A thankless task. Let us be steadfast in our resolve. In the name of our great nation, and in our people's name, and in the names of the civilized peoples of the world, and their nations, also great, we must resolve to be true and steadfast. Our course of action is clear: We must apply ourselves to the acceleration of this timetable, we must . . ."

collector of worlds

IN ALL LIKELIHOOD, the corrugated metal shed overhanging the platform hasn't been attended to since it was first installed, probably sometime in the forties. So the rain, which collects first in various dents and sags before making its way to the shelter's beleaguered seams, finds itself not so much thwarted as reconfigured: it drips steadily to the platform in a gridwork of determined drops.

Waiting passengers, who dream only of copious personal bubbles, instead find themselves forced to band together in little rectangular groups in order to avoid having the bottoms of their pant legs and the tops of their shoes spotted by the murky water, mingled as it is with the platform's distinctive brown-black film.

Accordingly, on rainy days people tend to bypass the station altogether, and it is home mostly to transients and jeering echoes. And yet, it is precisely at this station—on rainy days, anyway—that the train operators seem to linger longest. Maybe it's simply because no one passes through them that the doors seem to hang open for so long.

They've been hanging open for five seconds now, and still not a soul has stepped into the car. Which is okay with the six of us already here. We're living the dream, each of us set right in the middle of his own kingdom of empty seats, one of which stands to be reduced by half, were someone to come on board now. Besides, the open doorway offers a zero, a neutral X we can stare at freely, a welcome break from the hard work of stealing meaning from each other through sidelong glances at cleavage and hangnails, worn footwear and bald patches.

We're staring at the open doors, waiting—I was counting the seconds, before I got caught up in the sociology of the thing—watching swollen black drops land on the edge of the platform and splatter into the car, when the sound of hurried footsteps comes slapping toward the idling train.

It—my collection, that is—might have something to do with my pronounced artistic inability. *Arrested ability* is more like it. Asked to draw something—a tree, a house, an airliner, a human face—I would probably be unable to surpass the technical zenith I reached in the third grade. Two-dimensional line drawings, in simplistic front and side views, without a hint of depth or compositional acuity, that's what you'd get. Put one of these hypothetically current drawings—of a submarine, say—beside one drawn by myself at age eight, and the superior merits of the latter would be obvious to anyone. It would be clear, at the very least, that the grade school version was born from an as yet uninhibited fullness of the imagination, whereas its contemporary would disclose only ineptitude and self-censure.

It could be, then, that my collection represents an attempt to make up for this personal shortcoming. To compensate for a loss by making a fetish out of the very moment of loss itself.

A workable theory, certainly. But not one that throws my *interest* in these objects in the proper light.

The body behind the slapping footsteps comes into view. A union guy, maybe: layers of mismatched work clothes, white socks, black referee sneakers. Actually, he skids into view, skids right toward the edge of the rain-slicked platform—which I now notice hasn't been fitted with one of those cleated yellow safety strips. He's hula-hooping along in an effort to stay upright, and no sooner does his left foot gain the relative stability of the car floor, than his right slips into the space between the platform and the train—which I now notice is actually big enough for a man's leg to pass through. His right leg hovers over the space for fraction of a second, then plunges in, up to the knee.

It's a momentary shock for all of us. Undoubtedly, we're all thinking the same thing: the doors will close, eventually, and the train will pull out of the station and tear the man's leg off and blood will spray everywhere and he'll die and at the next station we'll be *detained* for questioning. It's a bit of a shock for him, too, I suppose. Though I now see my first impression was mistaken: he's no workman. Work clothes are of course something of a crossover genre, and on closer inspection his prove to be coated with the same urban grime as the platform. But it's the chapped face and shock of Beckett-hair, stiff with pollution and neglect, and the plastic grocery bags, a stretched handle still clutched in each swollen hand, that give him away as one of the aforementioned *transients*. And if his first few post-predicament utterances are any indication, he's like as not less sober than the rest of us.

His off-putting appearance, combined with the manner of his arrival, engenders a certain amount of confusion. Generally speaking, I prefer to let others play the Samaritan. I've skirted automobile collisions, crossed the street to sidestep an unfair fist fight, I've never any spare change. Still, apart from the wedged guy—who's only begun coming to grips with the process by which his face got so close to the floor—no one moves. So it is that I'm the first to help. I rise from my seat and move over to the doorway, thereby preventing the doors from closing—or so I believe—while I lean over to reassure the man, verbally. I've already analyzed his clothing and social standing—twice over, at that—and he's just now coming to the realization that he's in a bit more of a jam than the kind usually presented by his undoubtedly frequent diggers.

A couple of the other passengers, their everyday-hero programs finally uploaded, step past me and onto the platform, in order to alert the operator.

The first item in my collection was also the easiest to come by. It's no coincidence. It would never have occurred to me to start the collection were it not for the accidental ease with which I acquired that first piece. In the *catalogue raisonné* of my collection, I refer to it simply as *The Notepad*.

At surface level, directly above my local subway stop, sits is a brick-lined walk that intersects, after a couple hundred yards, the end of my street. This walk, which lies parallel to the underground tracks, cuts through the center of a narrow park, part of a larger chain of parks comprising a so-called Green Belt. Perhaps, at its inception, the unassuming plot delivered on the bucolic ideal promised in some landscape architect's color-pencil presentation. But by the time I moved here, years ago, it had already been absorbed into the urban fabric, the walk lined with the kind of trees no one would even dream of hugging, the thin covering of grass worn mostly to dust and riddled with the strategically placed turds of dogs and school children.

Halfway along this infernal promenade sits the terminus of a large subway ventilation shaft, a raised concrete collar in which is set a heavy metal grill. Apart from being an ideal spot for the relinquishing of consciousness, the vent is perfectly suited to the thermoregulatory needs of the local substance-abusing schizophrenics' reptilian lifestyle: it vents a steady stream of warm air in the winter and cool air in the summer.

One summer day, it must be five years ago now, I happened to be walking past this shaft. One of the lizard people was dutifully passed out on the grill, in a half fetal/half crime scene position. Nearing the guy I slowed, as I always do whenever I come across such mounds of prone oblivion, strewn about our parks and transit stations, human bodies so impossibly inert it's only natural, at first, to take them for dead. Who knows how long this guy had been thus exposed to the elements and his fellow man? His body was freshly and uniformly sunburned—including, I noticed with distaste, a purpled testicle that had dribbled from the right side of his cutoffs—so it must have been at least a couple of hours. Near his head lay a box of powdered donuts, half-eaten, and a knocked-over bottle of Sour Apple schnapps, its syrupy contents spilled down the side of the concrete collar to the ground, where it had congealed in a tacky green puddle. But the thing that most caught my eye was a blue, 6"x4" spiral notepad—the kind that simply says *6"x4" Spiral Notepad* on the cover—thickly crisscrossed by countless rubber bands, lying in the open palm of the guy's right hand.

This admittedly commonplace object projected some seriously totemic emanations. It might have been the thick cruciform of reddish-pink rubber bands (which proved, on closer inspection to be complexly interwoven). Or maybe it somehow tapped into that same thirst for forbidden knowledge that compels one to read another's diary or peek through bedroom windows. Whatever it was, the thing reeked of significance. It spoke to me. It called to me, the way a poor child, convinced that he is in fact the long lost scion of a noble family, calls out to the invisible agents of fate for deliverance and restoration. *Take me away from this life of vagrancy and into your own care,* the rubber-encased notebook said to me. I didn't hesitate. After a quick scan of the park to see that we were otherwise alone, I stepped over to where the guy lay, reached down and took the notepad.

I'm leaning over the wedged guy—he's still embarrassed, mostly, he wants us to understand that he's never been stuck on the side of a train before—and part of me is asking him if he's OK and presenting him with the whole repertoire of concerned yet reassuring facial expressions, while a more important part of me is ogling the contents of his grocery bags.

Inside each bag lies a large, leather-bound volume, antique scrapbooks or almanacs by the looks of it, covers worn and water spotted, the pages, stiffened with moisture and pasted on bric-a-brac, fanning out sharply from the bindings.

My comrades in action succeed in capturing the operator's attention, and he holds the train while the three of us help the man out of the gap. I reach down in a clear offer to carry the bags, but, to my chagrin, he hangs on to them resolutely. We lift him by the elbows—one of the others actually crooks his hand beneath the guy's arm—and, once he understands that he must turn his foot x number of degrees in order to get clear of the platform, he comes out cleanly.

The doors close, and the three of us are left standing there, still holding the formerly-wedged, once-again-transient guy (I'll call him *Fwoat*). He's grateful, it seems, though he offers no comprehensible word of thanks. In response to our queries as to any injuries he may have sustained during his ordeal (pull a guy to safety and already we're thinking like police reports) he hikes up his pant leg and thrusts a knotty shin forward for our mutual inspection: not a scratch. Not a fresh one, anyway. The episode has left him completely unharmed. It's enough to kill off whatever charity the other two still possess, and they slink back to their respective personal-space kingdoms, now somewhat embarrassed for having helped. Fwoat, too, shuffles off, still mumbling explanations and excuses to himself. Then, drawn there like a metal shaving to an electromagnet, he heads straight for my former seat.

I feel a momentary sense of loss as he parks himself in my recently vacated spot: my once-limitless realm of empty seats, reduced to an earldom.

Even so, I sit as near the guy as I can without arousing the others' suspicion. It's irrational, of course—what reason could they possibly have to suspect anything?—but I don't want to tip my hand too soon. In any case, if anyone feels put upon by untoward closeness it's Fwoat: I've left only a one-seat buffer between us. It's a strategic move, one that comes at a heavy cost as, in so doing, I place myself well inside his ripe troposphere. But so what if he smells sour and I lose the luxury of some extra space? It's a small price to pay for the prospect of getting my hands on those books.

The Notepad in hand, I race-walked home, my pace quickened by the slight adrenalin rush that accompanies a victimless crime and by the prospect of sizing up my score. Once inside my apartment, I hurried to my desk and began to remove the makeshift lock. With exemplary patience—I resisted the temptation to use scissors—I eventually solved the tangle of rubber bands. There were two hundred and seven. I was about to sweep them from the desktop into the wastebasket, when I thought better of it and instead left them piled to one side.

Released from its smothering constraints, the notebook slowly expanded, until it was well over twice its former thickness. I thumbed through it quickly. Every page had been written upon. Good. I turned back to the beginning, still unsure of what I would find.

Phone numbers. The first five pages were nothing but names, addresses and phone numbers. I turned the pages: grocery lists, to-do lists, wish lists, appointment reminders. I had stolen the itemized, prioritized task manager of an average, everyday life. One like mine. Most likely, it had been discarded by its original owner before being retrieved, from the ground or the top of a trash can, by the lizard guy on the way to his picnic. And then I had come along and *stolen* it, a piece of garbage.

But providential encounters have a logic of their own. My hope was rekindled even as the disappointment and embarrassment began to set in. There *was* something strange about the handwriting. I looked at the first page again. Around the clearly feminine script was what I at first took for its smudged echo, or some strange filigree. On closer inspection, I could see that a commentary of sorts had been inscribed in the original text, in an infinitesimal and almost indecipherable hand. The tiny writing, in fact, was everywhere: traced around words and phrases, stalking the contours of individual characters, plaguing gaps and spaces. It filled the looped enclosures of Ps and Rs and 8s, hugged the serpentine curves of Ss, dangled from the sloping tails of 9s and lower-case Gs.

I took out my magnifying glass and examined the writing more closely. It seemed to consist solely of reflexive mocking and juvenile retorts. The entry for Roswitha Stern of 2A Thorndike Street, for example, was almost entirely obscured by a cloud of parasitic counter-text, a swarm of black-ink gadflies, which turned out to be the word CRACKER scrawled microscopically, over and over. Or, twenty pages later, a simple grocery list, the white space around it now so blackened with *NANU-NANU*s and *KLAATU BARADA NIKTO*s and other traditional *alien* slogans that individual words were barely discernible. Or a page of the original owner's vacant doodles—swirls and 3-D cubes and hot air balloons—utterly harangued by hundreds of *PIGFUCKER!*s, set down on the paper with such violence that imprints were left on the next eight pages. Or a wish list of books, surrounded by a flock of turgid, angel-winged graffiti penises, urinating (or worse) from all directions on the defenseless romance and popular fiction titles. Such, then, was the lizard guy's compulsive rejoinder to this obsolete organizer, and to the life it organized, discarded artifact from the realm of the mundane.

I restored the rubber sheath—with undue reverence, perhaps—and placed the notebook on the mantle. It had already become my most prized possession. Document of a so-called dissociative personality, narrative of a soul at war with Being. Or, souvenir of a parallel universe.

Fwoat is muttering to himself. He's completely absorbed in some arcane personal ritual for establishing symbiosis with his seat. He takes no notice of my intentionally proximate gaze; his concentration on the procedure is total. The incident with the door, it would seem, is already forgotten: *I won't be able to play the you can thank me for saving your leg by giving me your antique almanacs* card. I try to recall how much money is in my coin purse.

Finally, after a tedious and interminable exchange of self-remonstrances and attendant apologies, he manages to get comfortable in his seat. He places one bag on the seat next to him (but not, alas, the one between us), wedging it partially under his thigh. The other he sets on his lap. Then, with both hands in the air, he flexes his fingers, like a vagabond about to set upon a kingly feast, and removes the mysterious volume from the bag.

Without even the slightest inkling as to its contents, I know I want this book. The cover is not, as I had first assumed, bound in leather. It's actually cardboard, perhaps tan, originally, but now so perfectly honeyed with age and constant handling as to give the impression of hand-tooled morocco. The pages are thick and rough-edged, the ample spaces between them clearly indicative of the presence of some form of appliqué.

Fwoat's breathing quickens, as does my own.

He places the treasure squarely on his lap and once again flexes his fingers in anticipation. Then, with a delicacy I find alarming, he turns the front cover.

By any standard of judgment, *The Notebook* is hardly the most impressive piece in my collection. Far from it. But for reasons of sentiment—like those which a mother attaches to her first born—it remains my favorite. It was the first. And it was the easiest to come by.

It would be wrong to assume that most transients are alcoholics or drug addicts. This is often true, of course, but it is far more often not the case. So if you're going to start a collection like mine, you can't count on these guys being conveniently incapacitated, their works just lying there for the taking. As with any collection, most pieces will have to be *acquired.*

The hardest thing, if you are an otherwise modest person, is to achieve the appropriate determination of purpose. Once you have resolved to be direct and obstinate, the terms of acquisition usually prove quite favorable. These guys may not be at the mercy of some addiction, but for the most part they *are* destitute. Thus I find that a suffusion of the *numismatic aura* will usually do it; some of my best pieces have come for less than ten dollars. And don't forget, they're crazy, which can sometimes work in your favor. It's easy to get these guys to talk. Usually, they're talking before you even come along. Let them talk. Guide them, if need be, toward the object of their desire. Deliver them to that object while they are still under its spell (I once obtained a life's work in exchange for a shiny new cigarette lighter). A tug-of-war will sometimes be necessary. Remember that these items are rare, one of a kind. They will never be officially for sale, they will never be listed in an auction catalogue. You will have only one opportunity to obtain them. Be prepared to intimidate. Have an escape route handy. Try to avoid violence.

Fwoat brushes his fingers gingerly over the first page, a gleam in his eye. The sibilant bickering of his multiple selves softens to a mellifluous unity, betraying an almost parental solicitousness. I don't blame him. The surface of the page is beautifully mellowed, a deep, uneven yellow that evokes the passage of time in its crystalline form, the condensate of human contact: breath, sweat, dermis.

On the top half of the page, just off center, large characters have been written, in the blue-black ink of a fountain pen. The meticulously rendered letters, nevertheless unevenly spaced and punctuated by careless splatters, read: THE BOOK OF CLOUDS, VOL. 1. Beneath this title is pasted a glossy color image, probably cut from a magazine. A shallow white bowl containing a healthy portion of ravioli, floating like lifeboats in a steamy sea of thick red sauce, sits on the window ledge of a whitewashed villa, the shutters thrown open so that the dish might breathe in the fresh Mediterranean air and look out upon an azure sea, stretching out forever beneath a cloudless, sky-blue sky. At the bottom of the page is written the caption: MOSES AND MONOTHEISM (AEOLIAN MODE).

Slowly, Fwoat turns the pages.

There are no clouds in THE BOOK OF CLOUDS.

Instead, on the recto and verso of each page, numerous horizontal lines are drawn. Each group of three lines is spanned, on the far left, by a cosmic decorative device— comet, rocket, ringed planet—drawn in thick dark pencil, the arbitrary clefs of an imaginary musical notation. The bars have been filled in with more freehand drawings: additional celestial bodies, medieval crosses, runic neologisms, innumerable mandalas, and, I notice with interest, winged body parts, including penises (*collective unconscious?*). Amidst the baroque proliferation of designs are what can only be the *notes* of this strange composition: images of fried chicken drumsticks, meatballs, fresh ground beef, Shake 'n' Bake pork chops, burgundy cords of jerky, golden-brown fish sticks, all cut from magazine advertisements and pasted on the page with undeniably meaningful intent. As if all this were not enough, each page is bordered with impossibly complex arrangements of highly stylized miniature faces, drawn in color pencil. The overall effect of this *composition* is startling.

Fwoat runs his index finger along the bars, his fatherly cooing now replaced by an annoying but undeniably rhythmic sequence of sucking, swishing and gargling sounds, as if the mouth were the very instrument for which the fantastic piece was composed, the saliva generated by the savory clippings its medium.

Fwoat, in other words, is *reading* the book

The Notepad. Sal Correia's twenty-four volume *Proceedings of the Jovian Interplanetary Councils, 1848-2114*. Margaret Murson-Hellman's felt and avocado pit *Danza Cycle*. Lester Spivak's *Hall of Immortals (Graham, Bednarik, Hornung, Brown)*, shoebox diorama with bar soap, nail-clipping and body-hair figurines. *The Battle of Fortnap and the Ages of Limozeen*, ink, blood, skin, ballpark condiments and asbestos shavings on paper towel scroll. *The Book of Clouds Vol. 1*. The anonymous and the untitled. I place the works in my collection—bypassing most of so-called art history—on a direct line with the Paleolithic bulls of Lascaux and the theriomorphic *Sorcerer of Trois Frères*, with the *Code of Hammurabi*, with Hélène Smith's Martian travelogues and the extended family of Henry Darger.

Lascaux. For a number of reasons, the cave paintings—even the on-site facsimiles which tourists are now shown—affect us deeply. To begin with, there is the undeniable artistic sophistication of the representations. What's more, of all the figures—deer, horses, bison, bulls—only that of man, in the *Well Scene* (the only human representation in the entire cave complex) is poorly conceived, scrawled with childlike clumsiness, as though it were merely an afterthought or anachronism. It's as if, for Upper-Paleolithic man, the risk of death in the face of a charging rhinoceros, the ceaseless struggle of wresting a meager subsistence from a cold, implacable Nature, was nothing compared with the task of representing himself, of situating, *installing* himself in a world apart from the Natural Order in which he awoke. That, above all, is what strikes us: here is the only true work of art. Here, the world was conjured.

And then we realize that the human has but one true avocation: the creation of worlds. This is the lie of history, that we are somehow better than the old hairy, uncouth, squatting cave-painter, when in fact we merely work the world that he made like so much scrimshaw. The distance from the torch to the light bulb, from the *Venus of Willendorf* to agribusiness, is trivial when compared to that between the hunting of an animal and the omnipotence asserted through its magical representation. This is what makes the high-priced garbage in all the Prados and Hérmitages and MOMAs ultimately worthless: they participate in the great lie, that the continual ornamentation of the caveman's world is progress.

Sal Correia is true to the human calling. As is the sunburned author of *The Notepad* marginalia. As are all the other artists whose *work* I collect. They are not content to inhabit the world in which they arise. They're driven to create new ones. Carving out a novel, personal world from the symbolic debris of the existing world; a more impressive feat, in my opinion, than even that of the cave dweller disclosing the world in the first place. For the modern versions of that inaugural gesture exhibit the ultimate enhancement: each of these worlds holds room enough for one.

If my collection is a compensation for anything, then, it's not my lack of technique, of artistic ability. It's my lack of the power to create. Like the rest of us, I no longer believe in the generative power of my thoughts; they are in the service of the world that was handed to me.

I can't create worlds. So, in order to compensate, I collect them.

About two thirds of the way through THE BOOK OF CLOUDS, Fwoat came to an unfinished page. The bars and clefs had already been inscribed, but no *music*, and only on the left side of the page was the garland of faces complete. He brought the incomplete page close to his face and smelled it, first with short quick inhalations, then with one long, deep breath. He reached inside the breast pocket of his canvas work coat and pulled out a worn, cloudy plastic baggie, filled with small colored pencils. He took one out randomly—a rose colored one—and promptly set to work on the border. The tip of his tongue sticking out slightly from the corner of his mouth, he leaned his upper body far forward, his head turned, so that his eye was almost level with the page. He was completely absorbed, drawn into the page. Fwoat was in his world.

My thoughts turn again to the acquisition of the books. I have no idea, yet, what it will take. Money? Stealth? Subterfuge? I suspect it will take no small amount of compensation to separate Fwoat from his work while it still drips with his creative juices.

We're three stops past my usual station. We're the only two people left in the car. Nevertheless, Fwoat remains oblivious to my presence, lost in his work. He's still hunched forward, his face almost resting on the page. His posture reminds me of my own, long ago, sitting in a classroom with my arm resting on the desktop, my head nestled in its crook, lost in the creation of a tableau vivant, *Guernica* of some imaginary war: rumbling tanks and screaming mortars, formations of dive bombers raining down bombs and gunfire. Lost, not in the effort to complete the drawing, to create a finished product, but in the action, *the act of creation*, itself. Irritated, I suddenly find myself resentful of Fwoat, of his childish freedom.

My resolve to have his things deepens.

As if on cue, he looks up from his work. He sits up straight, sniffs, puts his pencils back in the baggie and returns it to his coat pocket. He closes THE BOOK OF CLOUDS, VOL. 1 without ceremony and sticks it, along with its companion, inside the plastic bag. He gets up from his seat and then waits by the doors, the same doors in which he was so recently mauled. The train pulls into the station, screeching slowly to a stop. Fwoat, still ignorant of my watchful presence, steps from the train. I follow him into the night, where it is raining even harder then before.

lint

TAKE IT FROM ME: YOU WILL NOT DIE. *Hold on.* I'm not saying you're going to live forever. I'm just saying that what's going to happen to you will not be dying, at least not in the sense you've always thought about it. It certainly won't be a continuation of what you've come to think of as living, I can tell you that. Not death, then, and not eternal life; something different.

Before I go any further, before I tell you what it's going to be like, you have to promise not to demand a whole lot of linguistic precision on the matter from me. I'm sure you're familiar with the shortcomings of language when it comes to conveying even the most trivial aspects of physical reality or subjective experience. How could it possibly be expected to provide an accurate representation of *what comes next?*

When I tell you, for example, that *somewhere between the beginning of your final moment and its end there exists an eternity in which you will find yourself suspended*, you'll just have to trust that I'm simply trying to convey the *basic idea* of what it's going to be like. Obviously, I know *eternity* is the wrong word to describe this interval (also wrong); it's entirely misleading, it doesn't in the least explain what's really going on, in fact it probably comes closer to expressing the exact opposite. Not that the rest of the sentence is any less suspect. *Exists. You. Yourself. Suspended.* They're all wrong; lies, practically. It can't be helped. All I'm asking is that you believe I'm doing my best to impart an understanding of the phrase *You will not die.* Not that I have to, either. I mean, when was the last time someone took the trouble to write to you from *inside* eternity?

Anyway, here's what happens: you're going along, living—happily or unhappily, it doesn't matter—when all of a sudden you enter your final moment, as innocently as you might turn a street corner, and find yourself suspended in the eternity that exists inside it. I don't mean suspended in the sense of floating, like you're turned into a gas cloud or something, or like you *become* a suspension; I mean it in the sense of trapped, stuck. You find yourself stuck inside your final moment. Not that it's somehow recognizable as such either; it would be equally wrong to picture yourself frozen inside some eternal snapshot or snow globe replica of your final *perception*. So let's just say—although it's completely inappropriate to put it this way, and probably counter-productive—that you find yourself transported *somewhere else,* where you also happen to be *stuck.*

So, you're not frozen and you're not floating. Instead, you're lying on a wooden deck chair, the fancy reclining kind like they have on cruise ships. You're lying on this deck chair and there before you, suspended (in the sense of floating) over your head is an enormous ball of lint. Because this giant lintball takes up most of your field of vision, and because it's slowly rotating, you come to think of it as something more on the order of a celestial sphere, a planetoid of lint. This is basically what the so-called afterlife comes down to: lounging on a wooden deck chair and contemplating a planetoid of lint. Heaven it's not.

But wait just a minute, you say. *What do I mean, exactly, when I say* lounging *and* contemplating*?* Good question. No doubt my well-intentioned but misleading choice of words makes it sound like I'm saying that in the next . . . *whatever it is* . . . you'll continue to possess, among other things, a *body* for lounging and *eyes* for contemplating. Well, as far as I have been able to determine, such is not the case. You have no body, no eyes, no obvious means of perceiving anything. My assertion that you end up lounging on a wooden deck chair and contemplating a slowly rotating planetoid of lint is not based on empirical observation per se, it just comes the closest to describing how the whole setup would have struck to me in the old days, back when I had actual senses. For all I know, you have some other kind of body here, some other manner of eyes. Anything's possible.

But I'm off-track. The important thing is, if you're willing to work at it a little, you'll find there's more to this nether region than aimless lint-gazing. Lounging and contemplating are merely its basic features, its magnetic poles if you will. Eventually, you begin to make out additional features of your new *environment*. For one thing, you come to distinguish individual fibers in the big lint ball. Upon closer examination, these threads of lint prove to be your memories, recordings of the events and experiences that made up your life before you turned the corner on your final moment and found yourself *here*. By my reckoning there's a thread for each experience. Each thread, in turn, is comprised of two strands, one for the experience as it was perceived, one for the way it was subsequently remembered (at first the disparity between the two is painfully embarrassing, so much so it's almost impossible to bear; but you get over it eventually—*who's to know?*—and even come to take a certain solicitous pride in your former faculties of revision and fabrication). You can well imagine, then, the huge number of strands it takes to make up the lint sphere of even a relatively short life like mine (especially when you consider that each and every dream you ever had is woven in there as well).

Such, in any case, is your first discovery, the net product of your life: countless fuzzy strands of memory, woven into a dense and complex ball of lint.

Naturally, this discovery is accompanied by an immediate and overwhelming urge to *interpret* the lintball, to see it as a symbol, a work of art in the classical sense, the various moments transcending themselves and creating, through the sublime totality of their interrelations, a deep, perhaps even disturbingly profound, meaning. This impulse is only strengthened by the fact that the lintball turns out to possess a recognizable shape (mine looks like a huge asterisk).

Well, let me be the first to tell you: no such meaning exists. I have no idea how much time I wasted considering the question, since time, as you will have guessed by now, has no meaning here. I *can* assure you I examined it from every possible angle.

First, I applied the principle of proximity. Perhaps certain threads were situated next to each other, in many cases even inextricably intertwined, for a reason. If so, it should be possible to determine that reason. Once I had collected enough of these reasons, I reasoned, it would then be a trivial matter to identify the common thread running through them, thereby establishing the greater meaning of my life. Unfortunately, the following group of three interwoven strands turned out to be pretty much representative: myself, aged twelve, surreptitiously sniffing gasoline esthers in the tool shed behind our house; myself at a baseball game, squeezing mustard and pickle relish from small plastic packages onto a pair of shrivelled hot dogs; myself, dreaming myself in the act of transcribing onto a pad of paper what I took for the proofs to complex mathematical problems that, in my waking state, were quite beyond me (the new objectivity of the lintball allowed me to see that I was in fact filling the paper with well-ordered columns of the word *mediocre*). If there's some organizing principle that explains the proximity of these memories to one another, it escapes me.

The application of alternative hermeneutic principles— ordering strands according to chronology, for example, or by spurious categories of content, or by even by free association and random sampling—proved equally fruitless. At one point I considered making a detailed geological survey of the lintball's surface topology, but quickly abandoned the idea as ludicrous: what relation could an asterisk possibly bear to my former life's ultimate purpose?

The promise of discovering that underlying purpose thus confounded, it proved an easy matter to turn to other considerations. It's only your *former* life, after all. You're *here* now, so what does it matter what your past actions might have meant (especially as it's clear you no longer bear any responsibility for them). I began to wonder about my surroundings. What else, I wondered, is here apart from the asterisk-shaped planetoid of lint and what I now take for granted to be a wooden deck chair? *Is* there anything else here?

In the old days (before I turned the corner on my final moment), all I had to do to take stock of my surroundings was swivel my head around on my neck a bit, rotate my eyes in their sockets, breathe, taste, stick my toe in. It's not so easy here (no eyes, no head, no neck, etc.). I can't just roll over on the side I don't have and examine whatever's next to me, a situation which presents real problems to the would-be investigator of one's otherworldly surroundings. How could I expect to discover anything about the nature (to say nothing of the existence) of those surroundings if I couldn't perceive them directly, if I couldn't even look at them?

For what seemed like eons (again, *who knows?*) I made no headway against this seemingly insurmountable problem. Finally, I decided simply to act as if I *could* see it. After all, hadn't I already spent all this time gazing at a giant lintball? Clearly, even if I no longer have a proper pair of eyes, I do have something analogous to a *field of vision*. Ignoring the fact that I have no apparent body, I approached the question from an anatomical standpoint: I imagined myself as a large, immobile eye, connected to a standard human brain. They say a lot of what we *think* we see is actually the result of representations created by the brain: blind spots are filled in, stable patterns assumed, objects on the periphery hypothesized. I don't claim to understand how it works, but presumably the whole thing spares the brain from having to continually process information from two-hundred million light receptors, a task which would consume considerable brain power and probably make it a lot harder to do things like walk and talk and tie your shoes.

Anyway, what I needed to do was invert this process, to somehow ignore what was right in front of me and observe only what lay on the periphery. I made some modifications to my imaginary anatomy. I once again thought of myself as an eye and a brain, but removed the retina. No sooner had I done so than everything went completely black. I put the retina back, this time removing the rest of the eye instead. Black again. I decided, prudently, not to imagine away the brain.

Apparently, I would not be allowed any shortcuts.

So it was solely through a sheer force of will (which I must admit I was pleased to find I still possessed) that I eventually managed to stop paying attention to the lintball, to ignore it out of existence. Then—slowly, surely—the periphery, if not exactly coming into focus, began to resolve.

My first impression was of two white lines, one extending from either side of my imaginary eye to its respective horizon. The lines broke down into rows of white dots, which grew in size until I could see they were in fact . . . lintballs. Giant lintballs just like mine, stretching to infinity. Each seemed to possess its own unique shape—clover, football, ringed planet—and each was slowly rotating above a wooden deck chair on which sat a large eyeball, attached to an equally large brain by a fat optic nerve.

This was it then.

Eternity.

One in an endless line of helpless lint gazers. I hope you can appreciate my disappointment.

That's all I wanted to tell you, I guess. I mean, on the one hand, you won't die. There's something positive in that. It's what most people are afraid of, after all. You won't die, so relax, or worry about things that are worth worrying about. On the other hand, things won't be perfect. Eternity, like life, seems to be filled with hard work and disappointment.

Not that it has to be all doom and gloom. You just have to make the best of a potentially depressing situation. For example, after discovering that I was just a dot on an assembly line of disembodied brain-eyes gazing at meaningless memory lintballs, I decided to imagine away my eye, retina and all. I have to tell you, I'm beginning to enjoy the pure, peaceful black that comes with the absence of eyes and, as I never bothered to imagine ears for myself, the total silence too. So for now I can rest at ease, content in the knowledge that if things take a turn for the worse, I can always imagine away my brain.

About the Author

Will Lupens has worked as a forklift operator, software developer, lawn mower and surrogate rough-houser, among other things. He writes in Somerville, Massachusetts, where he lives with his wife and son and his two enormous ears.